PRAISE FOR

The Rest of Us

"These oftentimes deeply touching tales of longing, loss and emotional and spiritual anguish are striated with, and enriched by, their author's multivalent identities: Gay. Male. African-American. Intellectual. I enjoyed them very much."

—John R. Gordon, *Faggamuffin* and *Noah's Arc: Jumping the Broom*

"Guy Mark Foster's *The Rest of Us* is a bold collection of gay, African-American themed stories. Now thought-provoking, now poignant, now funny, now sad. Fearful. Angry. The panoply of human emotion and gay male experience are found here. One stand-out story is "Boy"; shocking in its honest blend of poetry and pain, the story reminds of Wright's *Black Boy*. "Ordinary Life" feels both Baldwinesque in its elegant prose style and reminiscent of Angelou's *I Know Why the Caged Bird Sings* in its mix of formal narration and colloquial voices. "A Type of Vampirism" captures the intensity of 'queerness' in the finest sense of the word. *The Rest of Us* is a welcome and much-needed addition to the literature of gay male and African-American – and everyday American – experience."

—Daniel M. Jaffe, *Jewish Gentle and Other Stories of Gay-Jewish Living* and *The Limits of Pleasure*

The Rest of Us: Stories

Guy Mark Foster

MAPLE SHADE NJ

Published in 2013 by Tincture, an imprint of Lethe Press, Inc.
118 Heritage Avenue • Maple Shade, NJ 08052-3018
www.lethepressbooks.com • lethepress@aol.com

Print ISBN: 978-1-59021-006-2 / 1-59021-006-9
e-ISBN: 9781590211632

Interior design: Toby Johnson
Cover design: Ben Baldwin
Author photo by Helen Peppe

This book, in whole and in part, is a work of fiction. Names, characters, places, and incidents either are the products of the author's imagination or are used fictitiously, and any resemblance to actual persons, living or dead, business establishments, clubs or organizations, events, or locales is entirely coincidental.

Some of the stories in this work originally appeared in the following: "Immortally Yours" in *Shadows of Love: American Gay Fiction*; "The Book of Luke" in *Brother to Brother: New Writings by Black Gay Men*; "Legacy" and "The Black Ant (Lasius Niger)" in *Sojourner: Black Gay Voices in the Age of AIDS*; "This Man and Me" in *Ancestral House: The Black Short Story in the Americas and Europe;* and "A Type of Vampirism" in *Icarus 14*. The material on page 169 is copyright 1992 by Martin Connell and originally appeared in the Notre Dame University periodical *Common Sense*.

Library of Congress Cataloging-in-Publication Data

Foster, Guy Mark.
The rest of us : stories / Guy Mark Foster.
p. cm.
ISBN 978-1-59021-006-2 -- ISBN 1-59021-006-9
1. African American gay men--Fiction. I. Title.
PS3606.O753R47 2013
813'.6--dc23
                                                                2012036955

...I learned
there is no tender mercy
for men of color,
for sons who love men
like me.

—Essex Hemphill
(1957-1995)

Table of Contents

Boy. 11

The Book of Luke 14

The Word Nigger 21

The Affair 34

Lilliputians. 59

Lasius Niger (The Black Ant) 68

You Get What You Pay For 73

The Rest of Us 93

Legacy 103

The Confessions of John-Paul Simmons . . 108

Immortally Yours 112

Ordinary Life 119

Congratulations 128

This Man and Me 137

A Type of Vampirism 146

You Must Change Your Life 156

Between Us 168

Acknowledgements 178

About the Author 179

The Rest of Us

Boy

SIT STRAIGHT, DON'T SLOUCH; TUCK IN YOUR SHIRT; pay attention when grown people talk to you; fold worms in half when you bait a line for fishing; throw like a man not a punk; run flat-out, with your bony elbows stuck into your equally bony ribs; don't bite your lip or swing your arms when you walk; hammer a nail into a two-by-four with your thumb firmly in place, if the hammer misses and you wallop your thumb, clench your teeth and bear it; hit back when another boy strikes you, bloody the little bastard's nose so he'll know who's boss; don't scratch your privates in public; hold up your chin when you speak; don't fidget; don't pout; don't place your hands on your hips, and people won't too easily peg you for the punk you are right under my very roof due to become; shake hands firmly with men; kiss every woman as though she is your mother—in other words, on the cheek; hold open the door for them, and as they walk away eyeball their reckless asses; wear your wallet in your right hip pocket, even if you are left-handed—the same goes for your watch: strap it onto your right wrist rather than your left; take out the garbage every Tuesday; mow the lawn every Saturday; wash my Ford on Sundays; feed that mangy, short-haired mutt your mother insisted I buy you kids nightly; be an example for your brothers to emulate each hour of every day; make your mother and me proud today, tomorrow, forever; be a credit to the race; discover a cure for something; win a State scholarship; to cross your legs, rest the ankle of one leg on the opposite leg's knee—*never* cross one leg over the other's knee, and people won't too easily peg you for the punk you are right under my very roof due to become; stare people in the eye when addressing them; this is how you get people to like you whom you wouldn't give the time of day to on the street; this is how you intimidate a cracker; this is how you intimidate a nigger; this is how you pretend *not* to be intimidated when in fact you're about to shit a brick in your pants from being intimidated; this is how you cheat on your wife; this is how you cheat on your income taxes; this is how you cheat death: every Friday drink a fifth of Johnny Walker Red Scotch, fuck your wife, beat your kids, then afterwards apologize and bribe them into silence by 1) buying your wife a knit pants suit, 2) giving each of your three sons a five dollar bill; this is how you grow from being who you are to being who *I* am; shake shake shake your Johnson after you take a leak, punch sissified boys who stare at your Johnson while you do this; always use a rubber when you "pokey pokey," the skank may have diseases (*But, Papa, what's a rubber?*); beware you don't get the little bitch in heat pregnant, all women want nothing more than for a man to knock them up; don't ever let a woman give you lip, smack her before you suffer that, kick the whore in the gullet till she shuts her mouth; look out for number one, Damn the torpedoes, full speed ahead; remember: screw a woman enough to keep her coming back, but not enough for her good time to rival your own, also never put your mouth to a woman's snatch, instead push her head to your Mr. Good Wrench, hold it there till you feel your nut about to bust, then screw her mouth as if it's a pussy; share with your close buddies the first and last names of every girl you've ever "poked," including those who laughed and turned you down—especially those; look forward to fathering a son yourself and passing onto him the same twisted values and beliefs your mother and I passed onto you—well, at least all those that I did; *fuck* what your mother told you; absolve yourself of all guilt in your efforts at child-rearing, as I've absolved myself, as my father absolved himself before me; refuse the role of scapegoat in other people's life dramas, it's unmanly, and people won't too easily peg you for the punk you are probably right under my roof becoming; never become a punk, even if that is exactly what you are already, instead fight it, slit your *fucking* wrists if you have to, leap from a bridge—or better, cut off your Johnson, *I* would, and though you can never be entirely happy with a woman, marry one anyway; deny yourself, live every waking moment as *I* see fit until I croak, then, if you see no other way out, do as you damn well please: lay waste to every fiber of your disgusting being; bend way the fuck over to better take a stiff one up the ass; this is how a black man takes a stiff one up the ass; this is how a black man takes a stiff one up the ass from a white man—watch *me*; this is how a black man takes a stiff one up the ass and *likes* it; this is how a black man takes a stiff one up the ass and hates it, but pretends he likes it anyway—if he knows what's good for him; this is how a black man becomes the punk he has always feared he would become, as his father before him became the punk he too feared becoming; this is how *I* became a punk; this is how my *father* became a punk; this is how *you* will become a punk; this is how a black man passes onto his son the fear of *becoming* a punk, as I've passed that fear onto you—you, who are *already* a punk; this is how to turn that fear of becoming a punk into *rage*; this is how to live a diminished life; this is how to survive.

The Book of Luke

I AM ALONE IN THE SHOWERS WITH AN older white boy. He has the same Bandaid-colored complexion as the painting of Jesus Christ hanging in my momma's house. His naked back faces me. Oh, I'm naked too, but he's more naked, because *I'm* watching *him* slap soap between his reddened hindparts, on the backs of his thighs, and over his heart-shaped calves. When I'm in the showers nothing matters but the other boy I'm watching and the water hitting my head. I come here lots of times. After my swim, I take extra long washing my whole body three or four times: ears, throat, under the arms, chest, stomach, and down below. This way I can see more boys.

It's these ninth-graders with shoulder-length, wavy hair that I like best. Maybe I should not think it, but when I watch them it's like that painting's come to life. The thing is: I don't have religion like Momma. Oh, I want it sometimes, but it's not there. This is the reason we left my old man, she tells me—he doesn't feel the Holy Spirit squirming in the dark of his soul, and he laughs too often for no sure reason. But I rode atop his big shoulders when I was little and I'd wave at the other kids to make them jealous because my father was always happy. Their own daddies were drunk or off in the arms of glassy-eyed, wig-wearing ho's. My father never drank until Momma said she hated him and was taking me away from his bad influence. He drank a whole fifth of JB Scotch that night and sat on the front stoop outside our building.

When he came back inside Momma cussed the day she ever married him. She cussed her government job with D.O.T. She cussed the pink silk dress he brought back from the war, with the pearl buttons and the white silk pants underneath. She cussed all her TV programs, even *The Flip Wilson Show*. They were all bad for the race, she said. No, worse; they were losers. And my Daddy was the biggest loser, because he was the cleanup nigger at D.C. General Hospital. According to her she was not a lucky woman. A person had to be born into good luck. You could not acquire it like red hair or a Lerner's credit card. This was something in the blood like the trait for slanted eyes and pretty feet. Parents with pretty feet have begot children with pretty feet every day the world over for generations. It was the same with luck. The Rockefellers had it, and the Vanderbilts. Lord knows Rose and Joe Kennedy had the lion's share of it, until lately. But Momma did not have one drop in her veins, it seemed, nor did anybody she was "acquainted" with. This was humiliation itself. She said all this to my father.

I sat listening in their bedroom, the volume turned down on *Police Woman*. I thought Angie Dickinson was beautiful. I especially like the easy curving of her index finger around the trigger of her shiny black revolver. It always gave me a small thrill when she would take it out, point it at the accused, and shoot: "Bang, bang, bang!" My parents continued to argue in the room the Christ painting hung in. This was before Momma moved it to where we live now, near the Olympic-sized public pool where I swim. When she said, "I hate you, Eugene Miles," her voice was loud like she wanted all of Washington to know. Instead of blaming her blood, her unlucky life was my Daddy's fault, because he cleaned up after "piss-poor, ignorant niggers living off food stamps!"

And then I was mentioned.

"Have mercy! Eyes, teeth, those rubber tires for lips, that child is your mirror image, only yours. He even walks like you, swinging his bony arms back and forth like he's happy. But he don't know the first thing about it. Just like his Daddy. But let me tell you something: Left to me, I *swear* his life will not be a carbon copy of yours, you *nigger*. No *Jeee*sus!"

This is when my Daddy hauled off and hit my mother, and she fell down. I heard her shriek then, and the bed I sat on shook beneath me. I went to the door of the bedroom and cracked it open. She was trying to get out of the apartment but Daddy held her from behind. She kicked at him and swung her arms and finally a wild hand smacked him in the eye and he, stunned, let her go. My mother ran into the hall shouting: "Jackeee! Lois Aaaann!" I walked calmly into the room and stared down at my father. One of his eyes was closed shut and he lay twitching on his back. The breath knocked out of him. He reached out to me, but I did not recognize that man and backed away. He was a stranger in my happy father's body. I could hear Momma jiggling the lock out in the hall, trying to get to the street. But the catch on the entrance was jammed and she could not release it. The stranger on his back heard the jiggling, too. He raised himself up and went after my Momma and grabbed her by the hair. He looked at her, and then back at me, standing frozen at the bottom of the stairwell. The whites of his eyes were cloudy and filled with blood and tears. He shook my mother's head from side to side. "I think she wants to get out, boy," he said to me, then turned to her. "That right? You wanna get out?" He grunted, and then, all in one swift, clean, expert motion, he shoved the crown of my Momma's head into the door and the clear glass shattered.

"Get on out then, you yella bitch!" he said. "Get the fuck out!"

Not long after my Momma and I moved to the suburbs, and I started coming to the pool. To tell the truth, I don't enjoy swimming. I hate that the chlorine stings my eyes. But I keep them open to spy which boy I want to follow into the showers afterwards. This one I'm looking at is new to the suburbs, too. I see him at school and with his parents at the white Baptist church we belong to now. But check this out: I'm not even being slick about staring at him, even though he might get pissed off and shove me into the tile wall like some of the other boys have done. He might call me one of those names. But I'm used to all of that now. None of it bothers me.

Sssh! He's soaping his feet: lifting up first one and then the other foot like he's checking for turds under them. It's funny—somebody dropping a turd in the shower! I have to laugh at this. Hearing me, this boy turns around startled, and he looks and looks and doesn't stop looking. It's like he had not expected anyone to be there watching him; but it's okay

because he recognizes a trait in me, maybe, that doesn't belong to anyone
else, but that is ours only—mine and his. I have never been stared at like
this. Never. Yellows and purples shoot off inside his eyes like tiny bursts
of soft light. His eyes have become the ocean on *The Undersea World of
Jacques Cousteau*—so calm, but all the while hinting at the mysterious
nature of evolutionary life. And lo and behold: His hair is crinkly and
dark like Jesus' hair, only it's more tangled, as if, perhaps, a seabird had
tried to lift his earthbound body into the air with his feet and, with great
reluctance, had to let go.

Out of habit, I tense my legs as he stares, preparing to take the punches
from his fist if that is going to happen—just like my Momma must have
tensed her legs when that stranger in my father's body approached her in
the stairwell. But this is the deal: He just flashes those eyes, his back to
the shower nozzle. The clear water jets out and rinses the soap from his
reflecting shoulders and the foam collects 'round his feet. I've never seen
feet and ankles so white. It's like he is standing on top of a thick, new
cloud and his toes, like cupid-fingers, are reaching out to me through the
bubbly spume, their voices whispering:

Steal away, steal away
Steal away to Jesus!

I notice, then, the tiny hairs that trail to his navel. There is lots of
hair 'round his thing, down below, and it bounces a little as the water
hits it. His is a nice, fat one, much bigger and hairier than mine. I like the
color of it—like the inside of a cooked hot dog. I know he is not going
to strike me when he smiles. I know this even though I am not looking
at his face, if you know what I mean. And all of a sudden I think this is
what would make my Momma happy: Jesus smiling at her unlucky son.
Maybe then she'll think I have religion and will let me visit my Daddy
for his birthday. I have not seen him since we left the old neighborhood. I
miss him teasing me about tongue-kissing a girl. I miss the stormy smell
of cigarettes and Wint-O-Green Lifesavers on his breath. I miss the jokes
about my Momma's crooked toes, though they don't look bad when she

wears stockings over them. He only said they did to get her to laugh with us, something we all used to do. She doesn't laugh anymore. She's a full-time prayer woman now. The walls are thin here, and every night I hear Momma ask God for the one thing she never had—a big house with a yard and a sturdy tree in it.

She and I live on the ground floor of a five-story apartment building here in the suburbs. Crab apple trees have blossomed along the sidewalk and in the small courtyard. But none of the tart fruit to fall this season, she tells me, will have either her name stamped on the ripe skin or my Daddy's name. And of course, I can just forget about my own name. "It's not what the Good Lord has in store for us, baby," she says. "We're meant for something much better than that. Amen."

I watch Momma faithfully lay a dollar bill in the collection plate every Sunday, the corners of her mouth tense, her eyes aimed on Heaven, waiting for the great mission to show itself. I sit beside her small body in that church and feel it quiver and rock with each hymn and sermon. What is it that she expects from a God who would let His only son be nailed through the palms and feet to two beams of wood? If anyone was born unlucky it was Jesus Christ. Nevertheless, He was able to proclaim before His death: *Blessed are ye, when men shall hate you, and when they shall separate you from their company, and shall reproach you, and cast your name as evil!*

It is this passage I re-read every afternoon I come home from the pool. When Momma sees the Bible in my hands she figures I'm gearing up to be saved any day now. But I am stuck in the Book of Luke for other reasons. I figure Jesus is directing those words not only to His twelve disciples, and to the devoted citizens of Tyre and Sidon, but I figure the Son of God is also schooling my old man and me, because of our own bruises, on the subject of forgiving those who hate us. You see, it's like this: I can't believe my Daddy is as cruel and unfeeling as Jesus' father, even though Momma wears a wig these days on account of the numerous stitches required to sew her scalp back together; but Daddy had been drinking the Devil's water on that occasion of violence, and he was anything but himself. I am convinced of this.

My father has to be a blessed man, like Jesus says, and since I am flesh of his flesh I, too, am blessed, in spite of what my Momma preaches. In 6:27 of this same Gospel, the Lord goes so far as to say that we should do good to those who hate us. And though that is a hard one, I don't fight those boys back who punch and kick me—especially Carl Brazerol, who it seems to me has his own problems, what with his bad teeth. I will admit that it sometimes makes me crazy as a bedbug for vengeance, but I am not bitter.

In fact, I'm happy this kid is smiling and not spitting on me, or flipping his goodies in my face like I'm dirty. Maybe his Momma doesn't like his father either and that is why he comes here. I just like the lazy way he stares at me like he's not afraid of dying on a cross because he's a believer in the resurrection, too, and all it means, just like Momma. For no reason I smile big at him then, bigger than I have ever smiled at any other white boy. My smile is so big my jaw muscles snap and my teeth stretch to my ears. I can't hear the neighborhood bullies shouting in the pool anymore. I don't even hear the shower running, but it keeps splashing at my back like a baptism or a wave from an ocean of voices.

And then this boy is standing right in front of me. He is bolder than I am. He touches his hand to my wet shoulder. A jolt runs through my body like an electric shock, but lasting longer. His yellow-and-purple eyes are dancing all over my naked ears, throat, eyelids, under the arms, chest, stomach, and even down below. Before I can stop it from happening the bones in my face shatter and my smile grows so big it covers my whole twelve-year old body. This white boy says something to me and I say something about his crinkly hair reminding me of the sun rising in the east. But I cannot hear the words. All I can be sure of is my heart racing along beneath my warm painlessly expanding skin. I am now a great, big, floating, twisting, turning smile. I am almost as big as my Daddy's smile when he's watching Redd Foxx on *Sanford and Son*. This kid is smiling, too, and then our two smiles glide forward and press ever so gently against one another, like twin brothers in the womb.

It is here that I figure the Jesus in my Momma's painting must be missing. Can it be possible that I've pulled Him down from the wall of one religion, stolen His unclad body into the room of another…and bolted the door? I cannot tell where I am, or if the date of my Daddy's birth has passed and it's another day, a brand new year, or whether I am older than my age now, or younger. All I know is that the Son of God is smiling upon me and I am whacking Him off with my huge smile of a body. This has to make my Momma happy, too, I think: her unlucky son's sudden conversion to a worshipping faith. And if it doesn't, I'm happy enough for the both of us. I am so happy I might let myself explode into a zillion particles of blinding white light….

Oh, *Jeee*sus!

The Word Nigger

ONE YEAR MY NINTH GRADE ENGLISH TEACHER CALLED on my best friend to read aloud from Ernest Hemingway's *The Sun Also Rises*. Bobby Lundgren, though bright in his own way, had failed a year, and was a year older than I was because of it. He had wispy blond hair, and a thin, bird's body, and for some reason—maybe because his blue eyes were the exact color as the seas illustrated in the back pages of my mother's King James Bible—I liked him very much. And he liked me. Besides, he was only the second person to ever give me a nickname; the first had been my real father.

My seat in class was next to his, as it had been since the start of the term. And when Bobby stood he looked at me cross-eyed to get me to laugh. But I was an honor student, he was the goof-off, and so I restrained myself.

He began at the top of Book Two, in which a friend of Jake Barnes, the protagonist, arrives in Paris from Vienna. Bobby took up the narrative as Bill Gorton, who is an alcoholic writer, tries to recount a series of events surrounding his last days in Austria. Because of a lingering hangover, he isn't able to recall the details accurately, and falters throughout. To my surprise, Bobby read the passage with great flair and comedic timing and everyone in our class erupted into laughter, including Mr. Sillense. Without breaking character, Bobby mock-wiped his forehead and continued. A few lines later, he suddenly stopped reading and lifted his eyes from the page. He seemed panicked by something. Exactly by what, I couldn't imagine.

Each student had his or her own book open to the page Bobby had stopped reading on—page 71. Instead of following the narrative, as

Bobby read, we had simply given ourselves over to his care. Moved by the wry animation, and surprise, of his performance, we had also been momentarily caught off guard. And as he apparently did, we felt paralyzed by the shock. For that reason, none of us thought to glance down at Hemingway's book to see what, if anything, had given Bobby pause. And when, after this disquiet, he tried to resume and couldn't, we knew something was the matter.

After this second attempt, Bobby ceased to speak altogether, and just stood, as if glued inside his blue-tipped sneakers. Some students took this as a signal to shift about in their seats. To my discomfort, many stared blankly in my direction. I did not understand at first, and so I stared just as wide-eyed back at them.

However, that morning was unlike any other morning in our English class. Looking about, I noticed what I had not ever noticed before. That day I was the only student of my particular race present: Sandra Robinson, a dark, pretty girl with long legs and a shortened torso, was absent, ill with a toothache; and the school track star, Sammy Lester—whose mother was from Berlin, Germany, and therefore white—was on suspension for allegedly smoking in the boy's lavatory. When it dawned on me that this was the likely reason for my friend's sudden silence, a chill settled in my lower stomach.

My only consolation, however, was that Bobby was not looking at me, too.

After an eternity, Mr. Sillense pulled a stained handkerchief from his shirt pocket. He wiped his perspiring forehead and instructed Bobby to take a seat. He would finish reading the chapter himself. However, before Mr. Sillense could adjust the strap on his reading glasses, a frail student, with flame-red hair, sprang up.

"I'll continue," said Fiona Brown, whose shrill voice startled all of us into wakefulness. "I like Hemingway. My parents own all his books: *A Farewell to Arms, For Whom the Bell Tolls, The Great Gatsby.*"

And with this, she picked up a few lines ahead of where Bobby had left off. Jakes Barnes was addressing Bill Gorton:

"Do anything else?"

"Not so sure. Possible."

"Go on. Tell me about it."

"Can't remember. Tell you anything I could remember."

"Go on. Take that drink and remember."

"Might remember a little," Bill said. "Remember something about a prize-fight. Enormous Vienna prize-fight. Had a nigger in it. Remember the nigger perfectly."

"Go on."

"Wonderful nigger. Looked like Tiger Flowers, only four times as big. All of a sudden everybody started to throw things. Not me. Nigger'd just knocked local boy down. Nigger put up his glove. Wanted to make a speech. Awful noble-looking nigger. Started to make a speech. Then local white boy hit him. Then he knocked white boy cold. Then everybody commenced to throw chairs. Nigger went home with us in our car. Couldn't get his clothes. Wore my coat. Remember the whole thing now. Big sporting evening."

After this, several of my classmates began to whisper among themselves. I felt prickly beneath my light-weight corduroy trousers, and I began to perspire subtly under my arms.

Finally, the bell sounded and everyone sprang from their chairs. Bobby left quickly. So did Fiona. But I remained seated. I don't recall what I was thinking. Certainly, my head was buzzing. Mr. Sillense stood with his back to me at the chalkboard, writing out copulative verbs for his next class. When he felt my presence behind him, he hurried over.

He was a man in his fifties, with thin, yellow-graying hair, and a small scar, like a scratch, above one eyebrow. Before speaking, he clumsily bumped the leg of my chair with his foot.

"Now, young fellow," he began, in a whisper—as if he didn't want anyone else to hear. "I can guess what you're feeling. I'm a Pole myself. What happened to our people in this country would fill a book. But we survived. Despite the jokes, the name-calling. You have to be proud, and not let words break you. We are all God's children. A leopard can't change its spots. And nor can you coloreds. Now get along to your next class, son. Don't dilly-dally."

When I failed to respond, Mr. Sillense adjusted his eyeglasses and wrote out a late pass for me. He placed the chalk-smudged slip of paper on my desk. Without touching it, I left the room just as the next period of students began to straggle in.

Then I saw Bobby. He was leaning into the glass-encasement just outside our English class, which contained the emergency fire-extinguisher and a short, red-handled axe. He was striking his head over and over against the chrome trim, as if trying to think hard about something he couldn't think clearly about. And his hair was in disarray. I imagined he had been yanking again at the curlier ends to make them less curly—something he did when he was agitated. I started to hurry past him, but he grabbed my arm so that my books dropped to the floor. When he apologized and bent to retrieve them, I kicked him in the ankle and he fell backwards onto his backside. There were other students in the corridor and someone yelled: "Fight!" At this point, Bobby leaped to his feet and went after me. He ripped a hole in the navy Banlon shirt I was wearing. And a tuft of his blond hair, to my astonishment, came out in my fist. Soon a crowd had gathered about us—I recognized Fiona Brown among the girls—and several of the guys jabbed their small, furled knuckles at us, and shouted ugly words. I was struck below the eye and my glasses flew off my face. Enraged, I rammed Bobby into the upright lockers behind us, and he kneed me in the abdomen.

Eventually, Mr. Sillense came out into the hall, along with Miss Ingwersen, our biology teacher—which embarrassed me, because I'd had a crush on her for two years, since seventh grade—and the two of them lead us roughly by the elbows down the student-lined corridor to the principal's office.

* * *

Bobby and I did not see much of one another that summer. Unexpectedly, his parents sent him and his baby sister, Susan, away to a co-ed youth camp, in Edgewater, for July and August. I flew south to visit my mother's family, in Huntington, West Virginia. Each day I'd been in Huntington, I had sat behind the porch screen daydreaming as my cousins played in the wooded field behind my grandmother's home. In the evenings, I'd listen to my cousins' excited voices whenever the fireflies they had trapped in mason jars would intermittently light up. They didn't like it that I separated myself from them. Once I overheard the youngest of my cousins ask my grandmother why I no longer played with them, as in previous summers.

"He's stuck up, is all," someone else suggested. "That's why he stays away from us."

But my grandmother defended me.

"When you gits older," she said, "you ponder things you ain't *never* pondered before. That's all Eugene's doin. Boy hasn't stopped lovin you children," she reassured them. "He's just growin up. Now, you all be mindful, hear? Give him his due. He your flesh and blood. What the Lord giveth, the Lord taketh. 'Member that."

After that, my cousins looked at me a bit mournfully, especially LexAnn, who was a year younger than I was, at fourteen. But at least I was left alone. At summer's end I felt sad, as if I had let them down. I thought I would never see any of my cousins again, or not for a very long time. And when I did we'd all be changed. We would hardly recognize one another.

* * *

By the start of the next term, things between Bobby and me had cooled. I would see him walking Fiona Brown to class, and carrying her books. His hair was longer. Also, he had begun to show the first signs of the severe acne he would develop in later years.

To my surprise, over the long vacation Fiona's body had also changed. She had rounder hips, if not slightly larger breasts. And when she walked, her short skirts clung to her thighs more suggestively than before. However, her overly pale complexion mystified me. I was reminded of a fortune teller's crystal ball, the type I had seen in the movies: Clouded, it obscured what was important ultimately to see—what could save a person's life, or radically alter it. Clear, it simply revealed what couldn't be glimpsed due to stubborn willfulness. Or just plain disbelief. I didn't know which way to best read Fiona: cloudy or clear.

The second week of October, Bobby and I each tried out for the school basketball team. I was cut before the start of the third week. However, Bobby made guard. As a consolation, at my stepfather's urging I joined the school chess club. I also signed on as a tutor, to keep busy.

It was during this time that the first sproutings of hair appeared on my previously smooth legs, and around my privates. A few strands even grew out of my ear. I thought of what the Bible mentions in Matthew about the hairs on a person's head being numbered—hair no. 1, hair no. 2, and so forth, but that nothing was ever said, to my knowledge, about the rest of the body.

I was not yet the age I am now, nor was Bobby. We were just boys.

One afternoon I stopped by the gymnasium to wish Bobby and his teammates a successful season. I told myself I would then leave.

But that is not exactly what happened.

In the gymnasium that day I sat down and folded my hands in my lap. Bobby and I had hardly spoken to one another in the year since our fight. I missed his smell, and his voice calling out to me where the buses waited for the students after school. "Eugene, Blue jeans," he'd call.

Out on the court, the players were arranged into two lines of single formation. Bobby was in the line closest to the bleachers, as usual with his back to me. Coach Lewis, with his coal black hair and handlebar moustache, stood under the backboard, a silver whistle between his teeth, holding the ball. From the back, I noticed Bobby's hair had grown even longer; it was not as wispy or curly, but coarse at the ends, and less clean-looking than I remembered it. He had also begun to part it down the middle, like the rock singer Peter Frampton, a man Bobby liked to think he resembled, but didn't. I had always preferred Bobby's hair shorter, and without a part, but with his bangs spaced evenly across his forehead: a bowl-cut, like the actor Lance Kerwin from the television show *James at Sixteen*, who reminded me of Bobby.

After a while, Fiona Brown entered and sat a few rows away from me. Glancing in my direction, she smiled faintly. Eventually, I rose and moved along the bleachers to sit near her. She wore what my devout mother would call a floozy's dress, with a single thin strap tied at the neck, and a cinched waist. Her freckled back was exposed, and she did not have on socks or hose. Also, the kind of shoes she wore left her bare, chafed heels uncovered.

Immediately, I began to stare at her. As I did, the edges of her nostrils quivered, and the high pink points of her cheeks grew fiery red under the fluorescent lights, like her hair. However, her voice was surprisingly calm when she spoke.

"How're you today, Gene?" she asked.

"Fine. You?"

She rested her fist under her chin.

"I hate geometry. What's an 'Isosceles' triangle, anyway?"

Her question startled me. I didn't know how to respond, so I just answered her.

"It has at least two sides that are equal, Fiona."

"Oh, like a church steeple?"

"That's it."

Her pupils grew large. A mischievous tone crept into her voice. "What about when all *three* sides are equal?"

"Then it's 'Equilateral,'" I said, matter-of-factly.

"'Equi,' what?"

Here, my tutor-training switched on. I took out my blue, multi-subject notebook, a pencil, and a small wooden ruler, and began in earnest to illustrate—for a girl I had absolutely no liking for—the various geometric triangles: Right Angle, Isosceles, Equilateral, Obtuse, Acute, and the last, Scalene, in which *all* three sides were unequal in length.

When I finished I wrote out the different names underneath the figures and held the notebook out to Fiona. "There," I said.

Fiona took the notebook from me and stared at it. I waited for her to speak—a show of gratitude, anything—but she said nothing. She simply handed the notebook back to me, with a shrug.

"Hey," she said, after what seemed a long time. "What's that French word for a three-way? Oh, you know." She gestured toward the basketball court. "Your friend out there *insists* you know everything? Well, prove it."

At first I just stared at her. But then, for some reason, I said: "I think you mean *ménage à trois*."

"Well *excuse* me for living!" she squealed. "Bobby's right. You *are* a brain. Still, betcha can't use a straight edge to draw this, Einstein." She took a deep breath—as though she were about to dive under water—and thrust out her inflated chest at me. "Not the x-rated version *anyway*!"

Unable to hold it, she exhaled all of a sudden, and covered her mouth with the heel of her hand. When she did her ballooned breasts returned to their usual deflated symmetry.

"I'm such a bad girl," she burst out impulsively. "You don't know the half of it, I swear. Isn't life a *gas*!"

For a long time afterwards Fiona and I fell silent. Then Bobby scored a lay-up out on the court, and, abruptly, like a Jack-in-the-box puppet, Fiona stood and cheered: "One for All and All for *Fucking* One!"

At this sudden outburst everyone looked up at her, including Bobby and Coach Lewis, who angrily shouted at her to sit down, which Fiona only did reluctantly, and folded her arms across those breasts she was so proud of. A minute or two later, she stood up again, then sat down: She just stood, then—as if she didn't know why she had stood in the first place—sat. I thought she looked bored. Nothing could hold her attention. Not even Bobby out on the basketball court. I can only recall one other time in my life in which I'd seen such an expression on another person's face. I was living in southern California at the time, the summer of my second great love affair, with an actor who has since died. I had been driving one afternoon on the 101 and, out of nowhere, the car I was driving struck a deer. Immediately after impact the deer's body swooshed up and over the hood of my car. At that moment I found my grown man's eyes following the arc of the animal's body through the air in perhaps the same awed and mesmerized way my boy's eyes might have followed the arc of a ball struck for a home run—that is, had I been fortunate to attend a National's baseball game as boy, which I wasn't. What I saw next was the contorted face of the female driver in the next lane, only slightly behind me, who had apparently witnessed the macabre scene. The woman's expression was an unlikely mix of terror and humility, perhaps at having been witness to such a Technicolor triumph of man over nature. It was this look I saw on Fiona's face that afternoon.

Then she turned to me. "My man's *fucking* great," she hissed under her breath, to avoid the Coach's reprimand. "Isn't he *fucking* great?"

I don't know what came over me. But I turned to Fiona and shook my fist at her.

"I don't know, Fiona," I said. My teeth somehow were clenched. "Since he's been *fucking* you, Bobby doesn't like me anymore. He hates me."

Fiona's features contorted and she leaped to her feet.

Just at this point, Coach Lewis blew his whistle. To our shock, the entire team gathered before the bleachers, facing us, as in a proscenium. For the first time, I noticed that all the players were blacks, except for Bobby and a tall, brown-haired boy with a severe overbite, named Carl Brazerol. I found the too sudden awareness of what had previously seemed a minor difference between them devastating. I felt all the boys' eyes light on Fiona and then on me. Only Bobby looked away.

Then Fiona shouted: "You're a joke, man! Why don't you go live in the jungle with the other wild hyenas? No kidding, *sambo*! Go back to where you belong! We don't want you here! Never did! Not me, not Bobby, not anyone!"

I looked at her, and I imagined scribbled across her forehead, as in Revelations: **Mystery, Babylon the Great, The Mother of Harlots and Abominations of the Earth.** She looked, to me, wanton, with seven heads and ten horns piercing her scalp and angling out toward us. Surely, this was what had been concealed all the while behind the fog of her pale complexion: the force of her wrath, which would, I was convinced, bring about the sudden, and irreversible, end of the world.

For a moment Fiona cradled her head in her hands, as if in real anguish, and I felt a quick, but fleeting, impulse to go to her. But I remained where I was. However, she raised her head then, and resumed her raging. I wanted her to stop, but I knew I couldn't force her. It was the same as if someone were sleepwalking: I had been told that you were not to wake them—for then they might harm themselves, or you; instead, you could only watch, and if possible steer them to safety. The best I could do was to be her witness.

It was all anyone could do.

She looked out at the players, dressed in their damp shorts and singlets; then at Bobby, with his blond hair matted down the back of his scrawny neck.

"I know what you all want!" she continued. There was an odd torquing-motion of her face, like I'd seen Bobby's face do after he'd read aloud to us that day in class. "Don't think I'm an ignoramus! The price of our homes are going down because of you people! My parents told me! But you—you—you—*savages 'll* never get what you came here after! *Never*! D'you hear me!"

At this last remark, her whole body went rigid. I thought that if I touched her she would teeter over. She would shatter into shards of pastel-colored, stained glass. But, again, I did not go to her. And I remember I felt bad about that. I watched Fiona Brown clamp her hand over her mouth like before, as if to prevent something from escaping, or to hold something of dubious value inside. She tilted her chin upwards, and for a moment appeared to fix her eyes on the sunlight streaming through the high gymnasium windows. It was as if she briefly saw something there: perhaps a septet of plague-carrying angels, as is written in the Bible. I glanced at Carl, a boy I had tutored in math, and at a couple of the other players I recalled, just then, having seen by the Little Patuxent River the previous summer, with their families. All of these boys, I realized with a shock, with the exception of Carl, were different from the other students, as I too was different, in a way that actually mattered to people—at least to people like Fiona, her family, and their friends.

We were, all of us, then, silent, as if weighted down with thoughts, feelings, impressions, we dared not consider too deeply.

Minutes passed.

Finally, Fiona gathered up her books—her geometry text among them—and ran out of the gym, her loose heels flapping absurdly behind her. The thought occurred to me that I should follow her, perhaps smash my fist into her as I'd done to Bobby that day, or as Bill Gorton's boxer had done to his opponent in the story by Hemingway—for not allowing him to have his say. I told myself, at least I'd have my revenge. But, deep down, I wasn't that sort of person.

On that day, in the fall of 1975, I was much too preoccupied with other things—things which seem to me to have been all along connected, however abstractly, to my life as a boy of divorced parents, as well as to being a descendant of a people who had often suffered unfairly because of their origins, and too, because of the dark color of their skin. To complicate matters, I was a boy who would mature differently from other boys. In time, that is, I would find myself drawn romantically, and sexually, to my male peers, in the way that most of these boys, when they aged, would be drawn to women and not to each other. Because of all these things I would stand, in years to come, always at a great, great, suspicious remove from other people—just as I stood, at that time, as a fifteen year old, at a great, great, suspicious, remove from books.

I watched the players that day gather up their bright blue and gold warm-ups—our school colors—and file off the court quickly to hit the showers.

Alone, I sat with my multi-subject notebook open on my lap and glanced down at the geometric figures I had earlier drawn for Fiona. The clean lines and angles had for years been a kind of arrogant refuge for me. The precision of this type of wordless language represented knowledge. And I felt a tangible superiority and comfort in being able to understand something others understood less well, or not at all. Like Fiona, for example.

But apparently this was no longer enough.

As a last effort, I tore out the page of triangles and held it up to the fading gymnasium light. I stared at the illuminated images. However, all I saw was a confusion of blurred colors and edges—some vertical and bursting with red, others on their sides in opalescent yellow, or else at sharp, ascenting, blued angles. Each line had an apparent beginning and an end, which extended beyond the page, to infinity. Christ was reputed to have said: "I am the Resurrection and the Light," and it occurred to me, then, that in actuality there were no true triangles, nor a true faith, just as there were no true colors, black or white, but only vibrating waves of energy, culminating in a spectrum of hues. A person had to trust the particular kind and quality of his or her response to such visual stimuli, which couldn't be false (because it couldn't be wrong), and let that be one's guide.

I picked up my books and my ruler lying next to me on the wooden bench. And following the arc the shafts of red, yellow and blue light made beaming through the high windows, I climbed to the topmost bleacher. Minutes before, the entire basketball team had been running up and down the court—engaged in what, in my envy, I had condemned as a silly, adolescent game. I imagined Coach Lewis gathering his breath to blow sharply into his polished silver whistle. I imagined the athletes responding to this signal, and springing their bodies forward after the loosed ball. I imagined myself watching all of them, and trying to guess at what each of those boys knew about the lives given them—but which had yet to be revealed—and just what they didn't know but longed to, and which they were greatly, greatly anxious about, as I was greatly, greatly anxious myself about my own life. As Fiona must have been anxious about her own. As were my parents too, including my real Dad—a man who had troubles, but who, the last I had heard, was trying the best he could to reverse his bad luck. I admired that. The effort to take yourself further, to a self you doubted you could become, but thought nonetheless long and hard about achieving, if only because to do so would make you happier than you'd ever been.

That night I went home and greeted my mother and my new stepfather, a man who had been fair to me, but who I hadn't as yet warmed up to; my two younger brothers, CeeCee and Brian, who were ten and eleven years old, respectively, and whom I have tried to think very little about over the years, if only because to think of them has meant to think about myself, and of the effects this shared past may have had on each of us. They were all sitting at the dining table playing a game of cards, and smiling at one another from behind their concealed hands. And when I hung my windbreaker on the coat-rack, and entered, they all raised their heads in quick succession—one following the other, as if in a musical scale— and said: "Hello, Gene. How are you?" "Hello, Gene. How are you?" "Hello, Gene. How are you?" "Hello, Gene. How are you?" And then, in a continuation of this remarkable sequence, each once again returned his, or in the case of my mother, *her* attention to the game at hand. Not one of them had a worry, it seemed to me, that could rival my own. After all, both my parents' lives had already turned and were on the great, final ascent, whereas in the case of my two brothers, their lives had hardly entered the first curve of discovery. My own life, however, was just settling into its first, early sign of a pattern. I knew only this: That I was in the great, colorful, swelling center of it. I had no idea of where my own responses would take me. I only hoped away, and far.

The Affair

AT WHEATON COLLEGE, SOMEONE HAD DRAPED A BANNER across the balcony in Bal-Four Hood posing the following question: *American Intervention in Somalia: Right or Wrong?* Underneath the banner a throng of politically active students paced about with sheets of turquoise blue paper folded in half. Inside, in boldface, the same question had been printed. People were instructed to circle which answer they preferred, then to deposit the ballot anonymously in one of the receptacles provided for that purpose. Mark Henson rushed into the Commons, bypassing the excitement, and headed directly for his campus post box. He found inside campus junk mail, his credit card bill, and a white envelope with his name and box number scribbled in green ink across the front. He tore open the envelope and read:

> Dear Mark,
> I never meant for things to turn out this way. Bethany's hardly speaking to me. Nor are some of my friends. I'm afraid Bethany'll tell her parents, who in turn will tell mine. What a mess that'll be, huh? Sorry I haven't phoned. It's been an ugly few days. I'm all confused. My feelings for you and my feelings for Bethany seem to inhabit two separate worlds inside me. It's as if the one hasn't a thing to do with the other. Crazy, huh? I don't want to feel this way. I'm a mess, man. I can't think straight—no jokes, please. I just wish it would all go away. But you're right—it won't. I'll

have to do something about it. Thing is, I can't lose
Bethany. I don't *want* to lose you, but I *can't* lose her.
Got that? She's everything to me. Earth, moon, sky.
P.S. I won't be on campus this weekend. Bethany
and I—if I can convince her—are going down to the
Cape. My Uncle Rick's place. Remember? He'll be in
New York for the weekend on business and said I could
have free run of everything but the booze. No one can
have it all, right? Have a good weekend, bud. And I'll
call you on Monday. Promise.

Troy

Mark folded the letter back inside the envelope. Along with his
credit card bill, he slipped it into one of the zippered compartments of his
rucksack; the junk mail he tossed into a nearby waste bin.

Steadying himself, Mark tried to navigate through the rush of students
gripping in their hands the folded blue ballots. He managed to take only
two steps before his vision blurred from the emotions swirling inside him:
the brightly colored fleece jackets, the patched denim jeans, and flushed
faces of his classmates all seemed to blend into a single panorama of
indistinct hues and amorphous shapes. Even the normally precise New
England diction sounded, to his ears, slurred and oddly unmodulated.

He needed a breath of fresh air. However, before Mark could reach
one of the exits, he heard someone shout his name.

"Henson, you going to lunch?"

It was Peter Frame, the student manager of the men's lacrosse team.

Mark shook his head. "Sorry, Pete. No. But I'm headed to my room."

Peter Frame was a woefully thin student from Bar Harbor, Maine,
who stood maybe 5'6", and must have weighed barely 100 lbs. Peter
made no secret of having joined the lacrosse team to avoid taking a gym
credit. He seemed to consider it a mark of revolutionary distinction: an
athlete by any means necessary.

"I'm starving, dude," Peter said, pinching the bridge of his perpetually sweat-slickened nose. "Think I'll go see what *Chez* Marriott has on the menu. Sure you can't make it?"

Mark stood firm. "Can I take a rain check?"

Just then, a woman student walked up and thrust a blue ballot at them. Mark shook his head, but Peter Frame took it and thanked her.

"You'll probably meet Evanston later, won't you?" Peter asked, stuffing the ballot into his backpocket.

"Hardly," answered Mark. "Troy's off to the Cape for the weekend, with Bethany."

"Dude, you can't be serious?"

"That's what he said."

Peter Frame laughed. "What a load of crap!" He moved closer to Mark, and lowered his voice. "Between us two, you're the best catch in *that* sea. Give Evanston time. He'll come around. If he doesn't, the son of a gun wasn't worth it in the first place. Right?"

At this, Peter Frame glanced over his shoulder.

"Besides," he continued, "you guys make a handsome couple. The best. Christ! The way I see it, Evanston doesn't know his left nut from his right. When he comes clean, he'll see what's been before his eyes the whole time. Hang in there, Henson. I've got a ten-spot on *you*. And I'm just gonna let it ride. Take it easy."

"You bet," said Mark; then, "Thanks, Pete."

"No sweat, man."

Mark was well on his way to his dorm before he paused to consider what Peter Frame had actually said. Had his strong defense of their relationship meant that Peter was also gay? Or simply that he was observant? Maybe it was all a practical joke, and Mark would find his name scribbled on the door of a bathroom stall in a few hours: "For a good time, call Mark Henson at 285-0641." How many others knew about him and Troy besides Pete and Bethany, he wondered? Had word *really* gotten around so quickly that the two of them had been secretly dating for weeks?

As he crossed the quad, Mark noted that few students met his eye. It was as if those who knew the whole story, or just a piece of it, had collectively agreed to shut him out. And except for the other black students—who, due to racial loyalty, wouldn't comment on the situation at all, nor shun him—they smiled weakly or gave him the cold shoulder; several students avoided all contact with him, as if he had a communicable disease.

But had Mark really expected *anyone* to be on his side? Troy was popular, and the captain of the men's lacrosse team. With his thick, reddish-blond hair and ruddy cheeks, he was classically handsome, and tall, though not especially muscular. His father had been featured in a recent *Fortune* magazine article, which had included a flattering photograph of Troy and the rest of his well-tanned family—his sister Chrissy, a freshman at Sarah Lawrence, and his attractive stepmother, who was nearly twenty years younger than Troy's Dad.

The idea that Mark and Troy were even friends—let alone anything else—did not quite fit people's imaginations. Not that Mark Henson, on his own merits, wasn't good-looking and well-liked. At 5'11" tall and weighing just under 180 lbs., Mark had the broad shoulders and tapered waistline of a professional something or other—perhaps a hat-check girl, one especially queeny friend had once quipped. During his adolescence, Mark had never played organized athletics; at the time, he had been too focused on academics, even by his own rigorous standards. Instead, he often went off by himself for long jogs, five to ten miles, along the main road where he lived with his parents, in Suitland, Maryland. At Wheaton, several male and female students had been secretly drawn to him. However, Mark hadn't shown a serious interest in anyone since his sophomore year. And that relationship had ended in disaster. He hadn't cared to repeat the mistake of falling head-over-heels for someone who couldn't fall head-over-heels in return with him, or with whom he'd have to sneak about campus in order to be alone, for fear of other people finding out about their relationship. Fortunately, Antonio Rodriguez had been a senior, and had long since graduated and returned to Guadalajara. Lately, whenever anyone queried Mark about his love life, he pleaded that he was too busy to think about such things. And being openly gay at a college that had few out students didn't exactly increase his odds of finding true love, let alone getting laid. For these reasons, Mark cultivated the most superficial attachments with his fellow classmates. Anything more would lead only to frustration and sleepless nights, not to mention poor grades. He couldn't let that happen again.

Peter Frame's response, however, *had* surprised him. It gave Mark a new outlook and confidence about things with Troy, which in several ways was little different, he had to admit, from his relationship with Antonio. Still, if someone like Peter could picture them as a couple, then maybe this one had a chance.

Once inside his room, Mark pulled out Troy's letter. He took note of the hurried scrawl, and distinctive slant of his friend's cursive style. Troy had once said that his poor penmanship was due to his biological mother having forced him, as a boy, to write with his right hand, though he naturally favored his left. Because of Troy's flippant way in telling it, Mark hadn't been sure whether Troy was lying, or if the story was actually grounded in truth. Like many of the more privileged students at Wheaton, Troy often said things as if it didn't really matter one way or the other if what he'd said was factual, or if it was made up. One evening Mark pressed Troy about this. The other man shrugged, and tried to change the subject. But Mark would not let it go.

"The truth matters," he said. "It's the only thing that does. You can't just go about saying false things as if they're really true. The same with true things: if something's true you have to say it is; if it's false, likewise, you have to say it's false. If we mix true things with false things, Troy, where would that leave everybody? Where would it leave you and me, huh?"

This conversation had taken place a week ago. The two of them had been in Mark's room, studying for a sociology exam they had in a couple of days. Troy stood up and walked to the window. He raised the shade a little and stared out at the students walking across the quadrangle; then, perhaps realizing that others might recognize him, he stepped back.

"I'd better go," he said, picking up his lacrosse bag off the floor.

"Go where?" Mark asked. He fanned the pages of his sociology text. "We haven't gone over the difference between Modernization theory and Dependency theory." He turned to Chapter Eleven. "Quick! What did

Rostow say were the four stages a country passes through on its way from a Third World to a First World society?"

"I don't know," said Troy. "You tell me."

"Come on. Take a stab at it. You *know* this. I'm sure you do."

Troy didn't answer.

"Okay." Mark looked down at the page. "I'll give you the first one. 'Traditional stage.' Rostow says that, in the beginning, societies are culturally fixed. Got that? Socialized to revere the past, the people in these societies in turn resist significant change—in this case, technology—in favor of traditional patterns of belief. Often spiritually rich, these cultures nonetheless lag behind others in material abundance. Okay, your turn. What's the second stage?"

Again, Troy didn't respond. He folded his arms across his chest and stared down at the floor.

Mark walked over to the window and lowered the shade.

"Okay," he said, resting a hand on Troy's shoulders. "I've had enough. You've been acting weird for a couple of days. What's the matter? Talk to me."

Troy parted his lips to speak, but no words came out.

"You worried about Thursday's exam? Is that it?" Mark dropped his arm to his friend's waist. He kissed the slope of Troy's neck. "Well, don't worry. You'll do fine. You know this stuff; your head's just all jumbled, what with that game against Babson today. You were great. I was so proud of you. Three goddamn goals in the last three minutes. Man, you were on fire."

At that moment a telephone rang down the hall. A student's shrill voice screamed out: "It's Jimmy! I know it's Jimmy! *Answer it!*"

Gently, Troy lifted Mark's arms and freed himself. He sat at the edge of the bed and covered his face with his calloused hands. The sound Troy made when he began to cry was unbearable for Mark; it was as if Troy were being tortured in some mean, sadistic fashion that lasted over several hours or even days. Mark sat down on the bed too, and draped an arm over his friend's shoulder. With the other arm, he reached across and pulled Troy's body toward him; they held one another for several minutes, until Troy quieted.

In a halting voice, Troy explained that his girlfriend, Bethany, had found out about them.

"I was writing a note to you," he said, wiping his nose. "A long, gushing love note. Saying how glad I was to be with you. How happy I've been these last few weeks. The whole nine. This was on Sunday. I put the note inside my desk. I wanted time to think up more sweet nothings to write to you. Because you deserved it. I hadn't felt so crazy, up and down happy in a long time. I wanted to celebrate the fact that I didn't feel bad about us. Not the way I thought I would. I needed to celebrate it. And to let you know my feelings. I guess I just didn't count on Beth going in my desk, and finding what I'd written."

"Oh, Troy."

"When she confronted me about it, I thought about lying, man. I really did. Saying it was for a writing exercise in old man Carlyle's class. You know, writing from a perspective that wasn't your own, in order to gain empathy with a character who was unlike yourself. Old man Carlyle's been giving out that assignment for fifty years. But that would've been calling a thing false that was true, as you say. I mean, it wasn't unlike me to write those words. I wrote them. And so I didn't *want* to lie. I wanted to feel proud. It's something to feel proud of, these feelings. Isn't it?"

That night Troy returned to his room, and Mark lay alone in his bed, unable to fall sleep. The next day, sitting down at breakfast, he found a note that someone had apparently slipped underneath his plate when he wasn't looking. The note read:

> Isn't nigger dick good enough for you?
> You have to go to the white man for your
> perversion?

Throughout the day, Mark noticed that several students looked askance at him whenever he passed by them. Once, after he'd gone into a stall in the lavatory, someone had opened the outer door and made a series of monkey sounds, which in turn were followed by obscene slurping noises. Before Mark could see who it was they had rushed out.

He wanted to speak with Troy about these disturbing incidents. But Troy had not returned his calls. In fact, the letter Mark had received was so far the only contact he'd had with his friend since Tuesday night's study session for Professor Tsien's sociology mid-term. And on Thursday, Troy had completed his exam quickly, then disappeared without a word.

Mark put the letter on his bureau. He noticed two calls on his answering machine and played them back. One was from his mother. The other was an overly effeminate, high-pitched voice asking for Mr. and Mrs. Troy Evanston; not surprisingly, Mark could plainly hear someone giggling in the background.

That night, Friday, Mark hitched a ride into Providence with a couple of the friendlier lesbian students, Sarah Leisure and Bridget Ross. They went first to Café Zog, on Wickenden Street, where they saw two other Wheaton students none of them liked and whom they decided to stylishly ignore. Later, they drove to Gerardo's, a queer bar not far from Brown. Sarah and Bridget immediately ran off to the bathroom to smoke a joint, while Mark ordered a Sam Adams and wandered around the club, trying his best to look self-possessed.

He had chosen to dress recklessly that evening, in a black t-shirt and what his friends liked to call his "fuck me" jeans, strategically ripped in the crotch and seat just enough to reveal what type and color underpants he was wearing—whether boxers or tighty whiteys. Before leaving, Mark had slipped a small silver hoop into one of his earlobes that Antonio had given him. When Sarah and Bridget got a glimpse of him, walking towards Sarah's silver Audi in the parking lot at Wheaton, they slapped hi-fives, and howled like she-wolves. Bridget, who was from Georgia, roared: "Honey, you aiming to cause a train wreck tonight, or *what*?"

The song playing was an early disco hit from the eighties. Mark squeezed onto the already congested dance floor. All around him, men and women dressed in brightly outrageous garb waved their arms in the air and shrieked at will. Others sang the song's lyrics at the top of their lungs, along with the female vocalist, as if the singer's message belonged to them too, and was not the exclusive rights of the music publishing firm. Almost by virtue of its enduring appeal, the song had acceded to being a universal property; by singing the words, anyone could enter into its world; man or woman—gender didn't matter—could take on the role the singer played: the lovestruck heroine, or the jilted old flame. More than anything else, it was perhaps this sense of being at a masquerade that Mark enjoyed most about going to clubs like Gerardo's. Here, he could be that wild, uninhibited person he wouldn't let himself be anywhere else, for fear of judgment or scorn, or even worse. Oddly, the same aspect Mark loved most about club life he also hated. He disliked having to travel to a separate world, as it were, simply to express this additional side of himself, and to avoid having to fret over his safety, or the safety of his friends.

Just then, from behind, someone grabbed hold of Mark's ass.

"Hey, sweet thing!"

It was Sarah and Bridget. They were sky high, he could tell. Sarah's red hair had turned a shade redder, and Bridget's nostrils seemed permanently flared for the evening.

Mark leaned over and tweaked one of Sarah's large breasts. She screamed and, in retaliation, grabbed at the lopsided bulge in his crotch. Somehow Mark successfully dodged this intrusion. And as a gesture of peace, he offered Sarah a drink from his Samuel Adams, whereupon she quickly drained it. "You cunt," said Mark, and lunged at her. But *she* dodged *him* this time, and in the process bumped into a frizzy haired blonde woman dancing a few feet away. The woman turned around, and smiled when she saw Sarah. And although Mark couldn't quite see Sarah's face, he imagined she responded in kind, because she and her new friend began, then, to move together, in an easy, sensual, woman-to-woman rhythm.

Oblivious, as usual, Bridget had already closed her eyes and was dancing dreamily in place to the music.

For the next hour-and-a-half Mark danced with several different people at once, ricocheting back and forth between his male and female dance partners, as if he were the pinball in a penny arcade game. Like everyone else, he waved his arms in the air and shimmied his shoulders and swiveled his narrow hips from left to right and back again, until his joints began to ache from the nonstop exertion. He decided to sit one out and went to the bar for a glass of seltzer water. There, he saw Peter Frame standing by himself, holding an empty shot glass. Mark walked up to Peter and tapped him on the crown of his head.

"Pete!" he said. "Funny thing happened to me on the way here tonight. Want to know what?"

Peter Frame stared drunkenly at Mark, as if he were staring into the face of the Sphinx. His eyes were glazed over, and not only was his nose slick, but so was his entire face. He looked completely wasted.

"What, man?"

"Well, I ran into a moose, a duck, a black bear, and Nancy Reagan. Guess which one told me to 'Just Say No'?"

After a sudden belch, Peter said: "*Dude*! You ran over a moose? Isn't that a felony, dude! You can go to fucking prison for that *shit*!"

Mark tucked Peter Frame's overlarge t-shirt back inside his droopy 501 jeans.

"Real sexy, Pete. How you getting home? You got wheels?"

"What was that, dude?"

"A ride? Do you need one?"

Peter Frame's eyes rolled up inside his high, slick forehead. He looked at Mark, seemed to recognize him for a moment, then his eyes once again clouded over. Mark thought to find a place for Peter to sit down, when all of a sudden Peter lurched, and he fell to the floor. Mark helped his classmate get to his feet. He found a quiet corner where he deposited Peter, then rushed off for paper towels and a glass of cold water. In the bathroom, he ran into a handsome dark-skinned guy with short dreadlocks, named Patrice, he had met last year at a People of Color LGBA conference at Brown. Patrice, who was from Haiti, was a graduate student in psychology. They shook hands, and Mark explained his situation—that he was tending to a sick friend. Before separating, he and Patrice exchanged telephone numbers, each promising to call the other the following week to get together.

When he returned, Mark discovered that Peter had fallen asleep. He collected Sarah and Bridget, though it was difficult to tear Sarah away from her new friend, and convinced them that it was time to leave. Each woman in turn groaned, but when Mark told them about Peter, they agreed to go.

The ride back to Wheaton was uneventful. Peter slept, while Bridget stared out the window at the changing leaves. Sarah drove.

Sitting next to Peter, Mark thought of Troy, and wondered what he would say when he phoned on Monday. Was it over? Did he lie to Bethany, say that it was Mark who had pursued him, when it fact the opposite was true? Troy had asked *him* to be his study partner for sociology. Troy had called to invite *him* to a campus showing of *Longtime Companion*. Troy had kissed *him* that first time. It was Troy who had said *No, I want to do this*, when Mark had said *What about Bethany?* and tried to end things before they'd really gotten started.

Though he tried to suppress it, Mark felt tremendously guilty about having deceived Troy's girlfriend all those weeks. Bethany had always been pleasant to him. He could not ever recall seeing her without a smile. She was friendly to everyone, even to those bigots Mark and his friends greatly disliked. It was as if she had not yet developed the habit of discrimination; therefore, her loves and her hates were all of a piece, and because of this she moved freely from one emotion to the next, one person to the next, effortlessly, fixing on neither one too long, but gliding in a smooth, seemingly right way between apparent extremes. It was this seamless way of moving about campus that perhaps made Mark envy some of his classmates, especially those who were native to New England. Born and raised for most of his twenty-one years in a predominantly black community, the campus to Mark often seemed divided into at least two distinct groups: those in which he was quite obviously welcomed, even embraced, and those in which, to judge from the behavior of many of his fellow students, he perceived an all too conspicuous antagonism. In addition, there were those groups in which Mark felt his status alternated from week to week—one day he was in, the next he was out; with these people, he could never quite manage to keep his balance. Quite often—this happened especially in the dining halls—he would mistake the territory of one group of students for another; worse, he might not realize this error until a less-than-subtle glance from one of them made his intrusion a matter of public record. It was for these reasons that nearly every individual Mark knew on campus—students, professors, and staff alike—had had to go through a rigorous personal screening process of his own devising before he could trust them enough to reveal any part of himself.

Still, Mark thought Bethany's way of loving a wonderfully liberating alternative to how he had loved and hated people before, which had been as either/or propositions: "Either you love me or I won't love you." His love for Antonio had been such a love; the same with his hate. When Antonio had refused to attend a campus-wide dance with him, for fear of being pushed out of the closet before he was prepared, Mark had taunted him: "Either you love me or you hate me. If you love me you'll go to this dance. Otherwise I'm breaking up with you." Antonio hadn't attended the dance. Mark went alone, and after being refused by one after another male student, when asking *them* to dance, he got shit-faced, and vomited on himself. The next morning Antonio wouldn't speak to him, in English or in Spanish. A few days later, Mark returned to his own room, a double he shared with a student who, no matter what he did, always managed to smell of spoiled milk.

Mark wished he could tell Bethany that, more than anything, he hadn't meant to hurt her. The first time between him and Troy had, well… had just happened. He knew it was a lame plea, but it *was* the truth. She had to believe that. He hadn't planned it, nor had Troy. However, a mutual attraction must have been present from the start. How else to explain the subtle ease with which they'd made love that first night, especially when no hint of their sexual feelings had ever come to light before? Mark hadn't realized he was even attracted to Troy until, earlier that night, in Mark's room, the hair on the back of Troy's hands had accidentally brushed Mark's when turning a page in their sociology textbook. The whole thing had been a surprise to both of them, equally. Maybe he just needed to graduate, Mark thought. He was anxious for the rest of his life to start; that could be reason enough to explain an attraction he hadn't been particularly attentive to, nor had designed. How else to explain it? But again, maybe he was in denial, and it was the real thing, between himself and Troy. But, either way, how was a person to know?

Sarah pulled into Parking Lot B and, as if on cue, everyone opened their eyes. Bridget got out first and helped Mark get Peter Frame to his feet. Sarah was beaming, and Mark looked at her out of the corner of his eye, as if to say, "Hey! I know why you look like the cat who swallowed the canary." But he didn't say anything, he simply winked at her goodnaturedly, and she winked back. Walking back to their dorms, Peter wanted to know where his car was parked? Mark explained that it was back in Providence. They'd get up tomorrow, he said, and—he looked at Sarah—if Sarah didn't mind they'd take her car into the city to retrieve Peter's. Sarah nodded that that was okay with her.

"Dude," Peter said, gripping Mark's forearm. "Somebody say something about killing a moose earlier?"

Mark woke at eleven on Sunday. Peter Frame phoned him a short while afterwards, and by noon they were on their way to Providence to pick up Peter's car.

The rest of the day Mark worked on an oral presentation he had to make in his Sidney to Marvell poetry class. At dinner, he saw Sarah and Bridget at a far table in the dining hall and waved to them. They waved back. It surprised Mark to find his friends seated at a table with a few of the students who had come up with the idea for handing out the ballots on U.S. participation in Somalia. Most of those students were white, he noticed; in fact, they *all* were white. He didn't know why this single detail seemed to jump out at him, but it did. He had seldom spoken to Sarah or Bridget about anything other than about being gay or lesbian—that is, when he spoke to them at all. He had assumed that, like himself, they had little interest in worldly events. Didn't their own personal affairs occupy enough hours in the day already, without having to think about which country was under attack by whom; what government was being overthrown by which guerrilla group? But Mark was also black. Didn't he think about that, too?

He finished his dinner and left the dining hall. Throughout the evening, Mark noticed a few students continued to treat him as though he were some kind of leper. But he'd had a good time last night at the club, and so he could ignore them and get his work done.

Before Mark fell asleep that night, Peter Frame stopped by his room to thank him. Bridget had filled Peter in on what had happened at Gerardo's, that he'd been ripped out of his mind, and that Mark had been a real sport in making sure he got back to campus safely.

"No problem," Mark said. He was dressed already in his nightclothes—a pair of plaid, baggy boxers, and an oversized baby blue t-shirt.

"Really," said Peter. "Most people would've just let me rot. But, Henson, you have a conscience. A rare thing as we close out the 20th century. Don't ever lose it."

"Thanks, Pete. Not that I deserve it, but thanks all the same."

"My pleasure, dude."

Before leaving, Peter Frame threw his arms around Mark's neck and held him tight.

"You're the greatest," Peter said, planting a soft, wet kiss on his cheek; then, shyly, he left.

The next day, Monday, Mark tried to forget the fact that he was to hear from Troy later. He had trouble sleeping and woke up at 7:30 a.m. He showered and went to an early breakfast, something he hadn't done in several weeks, not since Troy and he had started seeing one another. The pattern of Mark and Troy's sleeping together was entirely dependent on the shifting schedule that Troy and Bethany had worked out between them as to when one slept in the other's room. If either had a paper due the next day, or an exam, then each slept in his or her own dorm. Lately, as it was midterms, Troy and Bethany remained separated at night, therefore leaving Troy free to slip into Mark's dorm after 11 p.m. or so. For a couple of weekends, Bethany had had to return to Portsmouth, to be with her mother, who had recently had a mastectomy, giving the two of them even more time together. And because Troy liked to make love in the morning, whenever he stayed over Mark's room they had to invariably rush out at the last minute, to make their 10:30 class.

Mark chose a table out on the porch, where the sun was strongest and streamed in through the high windows. Few students were up at this hour, and so there was a comfortable hush of solitude, though he wasn't entirely alone. He took out his collection of poems by Donne, and flipped to the verse he had planned to discuss that morning in class, "The Prohibition."

Mark read the first stanza over quietly to himself, making certain he could stress the end rhymes without necessarily distorting the subtle logic of the poem:

Take heed of loving me;
At least remember I forbade it thee;
Not that I shall repair my unthrifty waste
Of breath and blood, upon thy sighs and tears,
By being to thee then what thou wast;
But so great joy our life at once outwears.
Then, lest thy love, by my death, frustrate be,
If thou love me, take heed of loving me.

He then followed the same pattern with the second and final stanzas. Finally, combining them, he read the whole poem from start to finish, several times, infusing each reading with a passion and intelligence he imagined the poet must have had upon composing it, in the 17th Century. John Donne was a poet Mark discovered he quite enjoyed. He especially liked the religious devotion to love in his much earlier Songs and Sonnets that he later carried into his strictly secular verse, and the poet's attempts to arrive at a practical philosophy of how one loved both God and men. Both types of loves, he thought, were troublesome to the poet—as they were to most people—and for similar reasons: that the beloved, whether mortal or beyond, was ultimately ungraspable, and yet each remained a point of immense, attracting light. It was within that light, the poems seemed to be saying, that we are all transformed and achieve our excellence.

By noon Mark had not only aced his oral presentation on Donne, he had also sat through a PBS video on Ida B. Wells, in his African-American history class. But still there was no sign of Troy. He did some research in the library until two o'clock before returning to his room to check his answering machine for messages. When he did he found a message from the Haitian student he'd met in Providence that weekend, saying that he had enjoyed meeting Mark again, and hoped they might get together soon for dinner. However, no one else had phoned.

At the dining hall that evening, Mark sat alone, reading over a draft of a paper that was due in the middle of the week. Peter Frame came over to say hello, but seeing that Mark was preoccupied, he respectfully left him alone.

The next day, Tuesday, when Mark hadn't heard from Troy he began to be worried. After lunch he stopped by Troy's dorm to see if his suitemates had seen or heard from him. When he did, he saw Troy with his feet up in the day lounge, watching an afternoon talk show. Seeing him, Troy jumped up.

"*Mark!*" he said, his voice high and enthusiastic. "How've you been? Good to see you."

"Good to see *you*. How was the Cape?"

"Oh, you know. Cold and wet. But it was great to be away. How was *your* weekend?"

"Fine."

Mark looked around the day lounge. Two other male students were seated on the sofa, boys Mark hadn't been friendly towards, if only because they'd seemed hostile to him in the past; perhaps he'd once stumbled into their group by mistake. However, they appeared unusually interested in his and Troy's conversation.

"Can we go somewhere and talk?" asked Mark.

"Sure, sure," Troy offered. "You want to go somewhere and talk, by golly we'll go somewhere and talk." He turned to the students seated on the sofa, and saluted. "Carry on, gentlemen."

Mark followed Troy down the carpeted corridor to his first-floor single. Closing the door and flopping down on his unmade bed, Troy again asked Mark how his weekend had gone.

"You asked me that already," Mark said.

"I did?"

"Yes."

"Oh. Sorry."

Troy's computer was turned on, as was his printer. Mark could hear the low humming sound of the motors.

"What's going on, Troy?" he asked. "When did you and Bethany get back from the Cape?"

"She wouldn't go," Troy said, matter-of-factly.

"You mean you've been here the whole time?"

A mound of freshly washed laundry was piled high on Troy's bed. As he spoke, he picked through the stray socks and began to match them up.

"No," he said. "Bethany went to her mother's for the weekend. I went to my Uncle's. I got back last night."

"Oh." Mark took off his rucksack and dropped it on the floor, near Troy's lacrosse bag. "You okay?

"Sure. Why shouldn't I be?"

"I don't know. Bethany, for one."

Troy shrugged his shoulders. He picked up a green felt tip pen and began to balance it over his knuckles, then tossed it onto his desk. Neither man spoke for several minutes. During this silence, Troy finished matching up his socks, and began to fold his t-shirts and underpants.

"Bethany's fine," said Troy.

"How about you?" Mark tried to touch Troy, who moved away.

"Don't," he said, taking a step backwards.

"Don't what, Troy?"

"You know what I mean."

Down the hall, Mark could hear the loud guffaws of the two guys in the day lounge, laughing, no doubt, at something they were watching on television. At just that moment, he wanted to storm out of Troy's room and quiet them; by force if they wouldn't otherwise. People like that had no right to laughter, he thought, unless it was at themselves. He wanted to believe that Troy wasn't like them, even though Troy seemed, just then, closer to the kind of person those boys typified than to the kind of person Mark had been convinced Troy was an outstanding model of: a person who didn't buckle under at the first sign of a strong wind, but who stood firm in the worst of conditions. But Troy wasn't that person; few people, in fact, were. Even Mark, to his surprise, often fell short of his own high-minded ideals. Still, how could he accept anything less, from either himself or others?

Troy neatly stacked his T-shirts, underpants, and socks inside the appropriate bureau drawers.

"You're saying it's over?" Mark asked.

Troy didn't respond. His laundry put away, he busied himself by clearing up stray objects off the floor and bureau and tossing them into his closet, or inside another drawer.

"Hey!" Mark said. "Am I talking to myself here, or what?"

"What do you want me to say?"

"The truth," said Mark. "Remember, that's always a good place to start."

Troy's breathing quickly became erratic, as if he were concentrating only on taking in new air, not on expelling the old. And the blunt features of his face gave the appearance of being sharpened around the edges. It was the way Antonio's face had looked that time he told Mark that he couldn't go to the dance, and that Mark should back off. But Mark hadn't backed off. He pushed all the harder—until Antonio, to save himself, had pushed back. In the end, Mark had lost the battle of wills. He had lost Antonio. Just as now, he imagined, he was losing Troy.

Nonetheless, Mark continued to push: "You mean, you don't want to see me again? Is that it?"

When Troy spoke, he avoided meeting Mark's eyes.

"Christ! You want me to spell it out for you?" he asked, picking up a lacrosse glove and tossing it into his closet. "Is that what you want? Okay. Just remember, you asked for it. Here goes: Beth's willing to give me another chance. On one condition: that I stop seeing you. Which means, no more study sessions. No more movies. No more slipping out when she's up late working to go to your room. No more anything. Got that?"

"And I suppose you said yes?"

Troy ran his fingers through his hair. "Well, gee, Mark. What was I supposed to say: 'Darn, Bethany. Can't Mark and I at least fuck every other weekend?'"

For a minute, Mark had a strange sense of déjà vu. Hadn't Antonio uttered similar words the night they'd broken up, except most of those words were in a language Mark didn't understand too well—not like now? Now, he understood everything Troy said to him a little too well. The coward! He picked up his rucksack from the floor and flung it over his shoulder.

"Later for this," he said, and turned to leave.

However, Troy cupped his hand on the back of Mark's neck.

"Just like that, you're walking out?"

Mark didn't answer. Instead, he saw a book he had loaned Troy weeks ago sitting atop the bureau, next to a photograph of Bethany—W. E. B. DuBois' *The Souls of Black Folk*—and retrieved it.

"I don't guess you'll be needing this, after all," he said, and stuffed the book inside a zippered pocket of his bag.

"Don't go," Troy pleaded, snatching up Mark's hand in his. "We'll work it out. I promise. Give me time. *Please.*"

Just then, Troy clutched at him. In hindsight, Mark couldn't really call it an embrace; it was too desperate. Troy ran his hands feverishly over the knots of tension that had formed over the past few days in Mark's back, all the while pressing his pelvis into Mark. Finally, he pulled Mark down onto his bed. He kissed him all over his face, hair, the back of his neck; he lifted up Mark's purple Polo shirt and circled his tongue about a stiffening nipple. Mark moaned. It seemed like weeks since he and Troy had made love, though it had been only a few days. Troy whispered: "I want you. I want you bad," all the while pressing himself into Mark, so that Mark couldn't think. He opened his mouth and slipped his tongue inside Troy's mouth, which was sweet and tasted faintly of apple juice. He pushed Troy off him and shifted his position so that he was the one now on top of Troy, holding down his friend with his own weight. In the past, Troy had only to say these three words—"I want you"—and Mark would drop any plans he had to resist. Like now. That someone like Troy desired him—someone who could belong to any one of those groups on campus to which Mark felt himself divided between, and whose members spoke awful things behind his back, or at least *thought* awful things, even if they didn't always say them, for fear, perhaps, of the earth opening up and swallowing them whole—that someone like that desired him, *could* desire him, had filled Mark with the greatest ambivalence. Clearly, Troy had deep feelings for him. But he had also denied him. All at once, Mark felt less drugged by his attraction to Troy, more alert, and able to clearly assess the situation and make an important distinction: Troy could never be loyal to him; he would be loyal first and foremost to whichever group he was a member; then, last, he would be loyal to Mark.

Mark tore himself loose. "Fuck this," he said, and quickly grabbed his rucksack and, despite Troy's protests, left his friend's room. His thoughts were swirling, but at least he'd come to his senses before they'd had sex. In the day lounge, with their feet propped on the furniture, those two guys were still watching television. After Mark passed them, he heard monkey sounds come from that direction, followed by the same type of suggestive slurping noises he'd heard that day in the men's lavatory. He thought to go back and to kick each boy in the face with the heel of his Doc Martens until he were stone cold dead; to take out his revenge on them at Troy's inability to want him in the way Mark needed a lover to want him, as if to harm those boys would be the same as directly harming Troy. He decided against it. Instead, he kept walking until he reached his own dormitory.

That night Mark telephoned his mother. She was pleased to hear from him, but added that she wished he had returned her call sooner; in fact, she had expected to hear from him days ago. Without thinking, Mark answered, in a rough voice, that his life was demanding. That she, his mother, had no idea of what he went through, day after day, living with these students, most of whom were white, and whose families were financially well-off, and who thought of people like himself—people who were *not* white and who were *not* financially well-off—as so much clogging in a drainpipe. These were people who had little sense of right and wrong, he said, of moral and amoral; or if they did have *any* sense of these things, then how they had learned to conceive of right and wrong, of moral and amoral, was apparently the complete opposite from the way he had grown up conceiving of those very same things. Just thinking of the weekend he'd just had made his *everloving* head hurt, he said. How dare *she*, his own mother, further add to his humiliation! How dare she!

Mark had never spoken in such a tone to his mother. But his mother listened to him, patiently and without interruption. When finished, Mark cried for a several minutes, and then he apologized. He confided to his mother that he was on the verge of a mental collapse. He didn't know how he would make it to the end of the year. Maybe he'd take a semester off; travel south to visit his Aunt Reba in Hampton. He'd always liked his mother's side of the family. Or maybe he'd buy a second-hand car and drive across country. It was getting too much for him, he said—

this place, these people. He had thought he could handle everything, but he was afraid it was all too much. Besides, he was having trouble sleeping. Not only that, but one afternoon, in his Human Sexuality class, he told his mother, he had laughed in the face of a white male student who had seriously suggested that people with HIV disease and AIDS be quarantined, to avoid infecting the rest of the population.

"I mean, really, Mom! Can you *believe* these people?"

"You *should* have laughed in his face," she said.

"Really, Mom? You think I was right?"

"Some things people say, baby, are just plain stupid. Shoot! They don't even warrant a response in words. That's just *too* polite. Sometimes a spit in the eye will do the job just fine. Thank-you-very-much."

Mark's mother said that she was sorry he'd had such a lousy weekend. She wished she could do something for him, but there wasn't anything. He had to figure out these types of problems on his own, she said. And he would. She had every faith in him. Besides, it would be Thanksgiving soon. He'd be able to see his friends and family then, people with whom he wouldn't have to be always on his guard.

"What about Papa?" he asked. Mark's father had not yet come to terms with his son's sexuality, though Mark had told both his parents he was gay at the end of his sophomore year, following the breakup of his relationship with Antonio.

His mother measured her words carefully. "Your father loves you with all his heart," she said. "You have to trust that, as I do. And believe me, Markie, I trust nothing else as fully as I trust my family's love for one another. Give your father time. That's all I ask. Can you do that?"

There was a long pause, in which Mark turned his mother's words over in his mind. Time? How *much* time? he wondered.

Finally, his mother broke in: "Oh. Before I forget. The reason I called earlier was just to say, well, just to say that I loved you."

Mark's eyes began to tear.

"I don't want you to be upset," she continued. "Nothing's wrong on this end. I've just been worried about you. I needed to hear your voice. You *are* my only son. And I miss you. Okay?"

"Okay, Mom. Miss you, too."

"Sleep better?"

"I'll try."

That night, Mark dreamed that he was an esteemed English professor, at a small but respected college on the east coast. He had a lover who was himself a successful painter and sculptor. The two men lived in a large, Victorian house they had renovated themselves, which had several rooms and tall ceilings. Plenty of sunlight filtered in through the windows during the year. On holidays, old friends would visit, so that their home was filled throughout the seasons with good cheer and warmth. A persistent brightness shone upon their lives, and upon the lives of all their friends, until the day they all died.

Of course, he would make it through the year; he had to.

In the morning, at breakfast, Mark saw Bethany Morgan seated a few tables from him. It occurred to him to go over to her, to offer his heartfelt apology for the course of events that had recently brought them together. After all, he hadn't planned the affair with Troy. It *had* just happened—without malice or forethought. But he decided against it. Several times he caught Bethany herself glancing in his direction, and then she would quickly look away. Instead, she focused her marble blue eyes on the thick, floor-to-ceiling drapes hanging from the porch windows, or on the mahogany wood molding of the high archway, which divided the porch itself from the main dining area. If nothing else, Mark was absolutely certain she saw him sitting there, wanting this small, consequential contact. But she refused to meet him halfway.

Something—he didn't know what—seemed permanently altered about her. She wasn't smiling. And he felt sad about that. She had recently cut her shoulder-length black hair to a shorter length, so that it now fell an inch or two past her ears—in a pageboy. The style matured her, although it too lent her features a more blunt, matter-of-fact quality that Mark found off-putting and severe; before, Bethany had merely appeared naïve. This time, however, her too-erect posture and firm features seemed to say: 'I have learned something about the world that previously I'd never known. Not that I care to know such things; I don't. But I can't *un*know them.

I don't know how to go about that. If I could, I would. But I don't, so I can't. And so end of *fucking* story.'

But it wasn't the end of anything. Not that Mark saw bitterness in her distracted gaze, but more like the faint beginnings of what some people might one day be quick to refer to as bitterness. More than anything, hers was the kind of expression, he thought, that results from having to admit that the treasured way you have had of perceiving the world—a way that had served you well for the greater part of your maturity—you now have come to find oddly no longer useful, even flawed. And knowing this, you then have the task of learning an altogether new way of perceiving the world, and those individuals who inhabit that world along with you. It isn't so much a choice, really, as much as it is simply a matter of deciding to go forward into your future, rather than to be left holding an empty bag, in the quickly changing course of what others, mistakenly or not, frequently call 'progress.' This was, of course, similar to the process outlined by Rostow in his sociological study of Third and First World societies. For instance, just as technologically primitive cultures were on the decline— like the Yanomamö of the Brazilian rainforest, who presently numbered only 12,000—so too were traditional ways of forming and maintaining human relationships rapidly undergoing modernization itself. If only Troy had been able to talk to Bethany about his attraction to Mark; if only Mark himself had resisted Troy longer until that had happened; if only Bethany had not gone through Troy's desk and discovered his note—a note Mark, now, would not ever get a chance to read, though he wanted nothing else as badly. If only there wasn't over a semester left to graduation. If only…

Later in the week, Mark went to a film with Peter Frame, who admitted that he considered himself a bisexual. However, he hadn't yet had sex with *anyone*, and so he couldn't, he said, say with one-hundred percent authority that he was more attracted to men than to women. Midweek, Mark telephoned Patrice DeLange. They agreed to meet for dinner on Saturday, then afterwards go to Gerardo's for dancing. Patrice was twenty-five years old; he had lived in the United States since he was an undergraduate at Boston University. His middle name was 'Toussaint,' after the famous Haitian revolutionary leader. He had told his mother he was gay at twenty-two, when he returned to Haiti for an extended visit after graduating from B.U. He'd had one significant relationship, he said, with a white student that hadn't worked out. But he was optimistic. "One bad apple don't spoil the whole bag," Patrice said, and laughed, proud of his ease with picking up American expressions. Before hanging up, Patrice told Mark that he had remembered his comment at the LGBA panel last year, at Brown, about the importance of loving oneself before you loved other people, even one's own family. "I liked that," he said, in his thick accent. "It stuck with me, you know. Right away, I thought: This is something true; it is. But it is something painful to learn all the same. We must all go through it. I knew what you meant, and I agree."

After hanging up, Mark lay in bed for a long time, staring at the white ceiling.

He thought of Antonio, in Guadalajara, a city he'd probably never visit, though he hoped someday he would, and he wondered if Antonio ever thought of him like this, with his head resting on his pillow, and his own ears straining to hear every word that was ever spoken in the world, and in every language people spoke to one another. More than anything, Mark wanted to be able to understand what other people wanted, desired, in their deepest selves, not what they *said* they wanted—that was always too concrete and therefore destructible—but what in their *hearts* they wanted and couldn't name, except when revealed between the lines and silences of half-uttered phrases that it shamed them to speak, afterwards or often during the very speaking itself. He thought of Troy's whispering to him at night: "I want you," and then, following, the silent retreat into guilt before dropping off into sleep. In the morning, Troy was always himself again, fresh-faced, boyish, and untroubled; it was a game to him, loving—one in which he both lost and won, depending upon the sex of his partner. Troy's sense of play was what Mark most liked about their time together; it was the reason why, in the beginning, he found it so difficult to put a stop to things, though he knew about Bethany, and already felt tremendous anxiety because of the deception on his part. But he hadn't been strong enough to stop himself. He wasn't *that* self-possessed. Not yet. And though he clearly sensed, after he'd seen Bethany at breakfast that Wednesday, that her newfound knowledge of him and Troy as lovers had pushed her, in some small measure, to the brink of something that, in time, would prove momentous, he nonetheless felt the anguish of the part he'd inadvertently played in her own personal…progress. However, he couldn't say the same about Troy. Mark contented himself, instead, with the hope that perhaps his friend would seek him out in years to come, when both had finally begun to flesh out their lives with hard facts, lives which now seemed so vague to him, and even slightly impractical. Perhaps, then, he and Troy might speak to one another from the depths of their hearts, as opposed to only their bodies. Following a crack in the ceiling with his eyes, Mark thought of a line in one of Donne's poems: "Love's not so pure, and abstract, as they used to say," and it occurred to him, in the dark, smiling, that Yes, perhaps not—but when was it ever, really?

Lilliputians

"IT'S DEAD FOR US," I SAID. "IT'S DEAD for me."

My feet were planted wide apart on the opposite side of the fence from where a dozen tennis players were aggressively batting balls back and forth over high nets. I touched the blacktop with my fingers, and then I pressed the heels of my palms to the ground to stretch my tight hamstrings. A saffron-colored caterpillar with thin black stripes encircling its wormy body inched slowly across my line of vision.

It was late afternoon, a Thursday, in July. I remember it well.

David, my lover of four years, sat at the top of a steep row of concrete stairs. He was thirty-one years old, a musician. I was twenty-six and did not know what I wanted to do with my life; I knew only that it was important I listened to him. But even though I forced myself, I could hear only the violent *puck* of the balls against the strings of the racquets, and the scuffing of athletic sneakers on the rough courts at 148th Street and St. Nicholas Avenue.

He raised his voice: "Richard! How many times can I say I'm sorry? The ball is in your court now."

"My balls," I quipped, "are in my pants, Mister. That's more than I can say for some people I know."

"Are you enjoying this?" His voice was calm. "Because if you aren't, what's the point? I don't know what else to say."

He offered this matter-of-factly, and so I stopped in the middle of my knee bends; but I refused to look at him. We had argued before, but never to the point of overturning furniture and calling each other 'sons of bitches.' This was serious; I did not want to love him anymore. But at the same time I was impressed that he did not lower his eyes in shame after what he had done to us. He was both a brave and silly man, and for all I cared he could burn in Hell.

A trickle of perspiration slid along my ribcage, beneath the t-shirt I wore. But I did not deserve the sweat breaking out in a river over my body. I had expended my energies for completely selfish reasons, and not to quell any unrest between us. David's own resoluteness in the face of his guilt made a mockery of my fair weather loyalty. This—though I could not admit it at the time—shamed *me,* not him.

Hence, I turned away from him and began jumping jacks.

"If you want to make jokes," he said, "I can do that, too."

"And a hardee-har-har back to you, David."

"I noticed you changed the locks. How am I supposed to get my things?"

"What the fuck do I care?"

"Hey, hey," he said. "Now that's enough."

I counted the number of jumps in my head and tried to keep my leg and arm movements coordinated. But my breath gave out. Soon I felt my face muscles stiffen and the blood gushed in a blast to my temples. I should have stopped then and stood toe to toe with him, worked things out. But that was an odd notion to me in those days; I didn't understand it.

After a while my feet began to land upon the ground too hard, and my knees buckled. Sweat ran down the front of my shirt and seeped in between the ribbing of my tennis shorts and jockstrap. My breaths were coming shorter and I drew air too quickly in through my nose, so that the insides of my mouth became sticky. My chest was heaving and tiny stars exploded before my eyes.

"What is it?" I asked, stopping. "Is it because I use too much teeth when I suck your dick?"

"Keep your voice down, Richie!"

I began to laugh. "Oh no. I want everyone to know I'm a lousy lay, and that's why you go elsewhere for your weekly blowjob." I shouted this: "*Eeeveryooone!*"

I could see Yankee baseball stadium past the Macombe Dam Bridge, and hear, under my strained voice, the sound of faint, electronic organ music piping across Harlem.

David Roane had had, in those days, a teenager's wiry, unassuming build: short and clean-shaved, with a tapered waist and small, expressive hands; but beneath all this I had reasons to believe an unrivaled vastness dwelled inside him, depths of wisdom and good will I would never possess myself, though I was a whole foot taller than he was and had recently grown a moustache, my first. And so when he opened his mouth to speak I tried to anchor my fingers and toes to the solid, dependable and singular brilliance of his white teeth, to avoid being swept away by his betrayal. But nothing he said made any sense to me. It was as if I was staring down the fatter end of a very large telescope, and so he became a foreign idea to me, and his voice, when I heard it, was indistinguishable from the puzzle of such a thing.

"*You're* my man, Richard Burrows," he said. "Let's go home. You're right to think what you think about me. Absolutely. I'm a donkey's ass for jeopardizing us."

Just then the rain began to fall. I gazed out beyond the tall fence to watch the tennis players file off the courts for shelter. When I turned to David he had gathered my racquets up in his arms and was waiting for me.

It was past midday and the sunlight had nearly faded. There were children playing dodge ball on the wide boulevard, and they flanked us shrieking and banging into one another with the wet, black ant bodies. David had on a red knit shirt and beige linen trousers. And although the rain was not heavy, the dye in the shirt would run and eventually stain the trousers. The rawhide of his expensive loafers would dull, too, and they would begin to squeak.

These things were important, I thought, not anything else.

Next to him, I was afraid that every observation I had ever made was superfluous, and, because of this, others were within their rights to see me as a completely trifling and petty-minded young man. Maybe I deserved all this.

"I meant to bring an umbrella," I said, thinking I needed to exercise some humility. "I guess I forgot."

"We're going to be okay, Richie." David was a half-step ahead of me and turned round to say this. "Rain is a good sign. It'll rinse away the bad feeling we had last night." He stared off into the mottled sky. "It'll help us to start over and to forget, too, I think. Yup, it'll do that."

"But I don't want to forget last night, David."

"You're absolutely right." His words came sudden and without so much as a glance at my face. "Neither of us can afford to forget last night."

I did a hop step and caught up to him so that we walked side by side. The chocolate brown loafers had not begun to squeak yet, but the rain water had coagulated on top of the Italian leather and would seep in slowly. What a pity, I thought. Also, his toes must have itched fiercely because of the woolen socks he always wore.

"Why'd you say that, David? How am I supposed to forget what you've done to *me?*"

We were not far from our apartment, which sat at the top of a steep hill on 157th Street, in a building Duke Ellington had once lived in. David slowed before we had to cross to walk up our street. He looked at me a brief moment and hugged both his arms about my tennis racquets.

"You've thought of me as this knight in shining armor who wouldn't for the life of him confuse a good judgment with one that was bad. And now that you realize I'm flesh and blood like everybody else, you hate me. My god."

"David—"

He held up the palm of his hand to silence me, and looked away. The street was paved on an incline, and I touched him on the shoulder to make him stop climbing the hill. When he turned around rain water lay sluiced on his face and the wetness running there gave him an utterly stupid look.

He tilted his head at an angle. "You don't know me, do you? I'm a complete stranger. Isn't that something? Me." He pointed to himself, incredulous, with my two racquets clenched under the pit of his arm, like hostages, and he projected that same incredulity into my body—into my limbs, torso, and cartilage—until I too was full of it. But it wasn't the pride of exoneration I saw in his eyes, but a helpless delirium, and another look I could not quite read, or else hesitated to. The tears and drizzle streamed down and intermingled on his lips, and I could do nothing but turn away from him and continue home.

That evening we lay atop the bedcovers not touching and I listened attentively to my lover, my first, breathe in the dark silent room. A beam of street- or moonlight shone in through an opening in the curtains and its razor-sharpness divided our bodies further into disproportionate quarters. It rained for hours, and I tuned my ears, too, as I lay there, to the accumulated water draining from the roof and splashing down the tin pipes outside our building. I reached for David's hand and tried to coax him toward me. But he resisted and rolled to the far side of the bed. In a short time he was sleep, or else pretending; I could not tell which.

In the morning David flung a relaxed arm across my abdomen. I moved in to him and nestled my head. It was still dark out and there was the beehive sound of the sanitation truck outside our window, and the worker's clipped voices. I had not slept well, and when I peeked across David's chest at the clock and saw that it was not even six a.m., I became very fatigued.

Without taking his arm off me, David said: "It's not your time yet. I'll go for a long shower and let you rest."

"Stay with me, David."

"But you'll get bags under your eyes and look like some over-the-hill disco diva. You don't want that," he said, trying to make a joke, which I ignored.

"I'll hunt you down and kill you if you leave me," I said.

"Oh, you," he said. "Stop being such a drama queen. It isn't you."

And then he began to tickle me and poke at my ribs with his stubby fingers. He pushed me against the pillows. I struggled, but he held my wrists and pressed all his weight upon me. I could feel his wagging erection slip between my moist thighs.

"What's that?" he said, smiling at me mischievously. He pulled back and let go of my wrists. I stared clumsily at him. He was so much more handsome than I was; I always knew this, and deep inside I was proud to know it. He was the original handsome man. I twisted his head between my hands and rubbed at his then stylish, fade-away haircut. I buried my nose there and tried to lose myself in his Egyptian oil scent. My eyelids fluttered and a bird-like tweak escaped from my throat. David rolled the back of his hand against my cheek and slipped a finger inside my mouth, twirled it there, until my tongue darted out obediently to take hold of it. I willed then for my morally desiccated body to be crushed and replaced, instead, by the far more eloquent gravity of his.

I waited. But I could not keep my eyes closed, and when I opened them I was instantly aware of my own arms, my own legs, my own chest. I was furious. My body was still my body. I could see only the disappointing, blunt tip of my own nose as I looked out at him. I could feel the tepid air splay from inside my nostrils and disperse across the bony contours of my face.

Our bedroom windows were half-raised and a breeze billowed the heavy curtains. I felt the light wind enter and skirt under and between our two bodies. All at once I wanted David to plunge his lean, angular sex into my moist bowels. I raked and clawed his back until he began to pant my name in a tumble of unintelligible, quick breaths. Finally, I felt the swift kick of his unprotected penis slip inside me. I let loose a cry and we vaulted from one precipice of our expansive bed to the other. At the exact moment it seemed I might explode and I would at last be free of my body, I thought: *But this manipulation won't work, Richie. He has to love you. He has to want to have crazy, up and down the walls unsafe sex with you. But he would rather be at risk with someone else now.*

I realized that he had made up his mind to leave me and that no matter what I did I could not stop him. I began all at once to howl like a trapped animal. Hearing my voice, David, as if in time-lapsed photography, awkwardly slithered away from me on his stomach. When he sat up his eyes were wild and the whites not white but a putrid glazed color. At that moment he was terrified of me, as I was of myself.

Our comforter was blue and streaked with fruity orange horizontal lines and David awkwardly wrapped his lower body in it. He did not shift from what must have been an uncomfortable position for his body on the mattress, but nor did he so much as blink in denial of the conclusion I had reached. He simply sat back on his ankles, not looking at me but more through me, to some memory, or future, that I gathered was all his own, and that likely hadn't a thing to do with me or with us.

I rose from our bed and walked into the hall outside the door. The white walls were a florescent lemon color from the sun and I had to shade my eyes. I wandered into the kitchen and placed the kettle on the stove and sat at the table. The rain had stopped and I listened to the noises beyond the window: the impatient car horns and the washing-sound of TGIF morning rush-hour traffic along St. Nicholas Avenue.

I felt weighted by my body, as if paralyzed from the neck down. When the kettle blew it blew until David appeared to lift it and poured the steaming water into cups. He brought my bathrobe with him and placed it round my shoulders and set the hot tea on the table in front of me, and one for himself. My eyes were bleary and my ass and the back of my head ached. I felt unpredictable and I was unnerved that David was in the room just then. He was behind me and when he opened the refrigerator door a chill raced up my back.

"Hungry?" he asked. "How 'bout I scramble us some eggs, huh?"

I looked at him, then I caught sight, through the archway separating the kitchen from the sitting room, of the untidy living area—the overturned seat cushions and the broken, ornate lamp I had smashed two nights earlier, when I had confronted him with what I knew of his faithlessness.

I felt I should eat something, and reluctantly I asked for a slice of toast to have with my tea. Before he sat, David grinned and pulled the window shades so that the sun shone fully in and brightened the room.

He said: "Honey, we can do anything."

I watched him in earnest ladle sugar from a bowl into his teacup and I tried to anticipate, as if our relationship was a board game, what insanity he would say after this. His eyes had lost the shiny, glazed deliriousness of the night before, but he did not seem at all sure of himself.

"What are your plans?" I asked, my voice light but accusatory. "You gonna set up house with this new buck, or what? I bet he sucks dick real good, right? Come on, you can tell me, homes."

The sun was behind him and he lifted his head to look at me. I noticed his lips were in mid-pucker from cooling the hot tea with his breath; and

I saw, too, the flat, streaked smear of my dried ejaculate from the night before, like a stamp of impossible ownership, against his forehead. I watched his hands, as if in slow motion, pull away from the sides of the teacup. The steam wafted up slightly from the hot water so that a small rain cloud seemed to cushion his unshaven chin.

He shook his head. "I'm not moving in with anyone, Richard. You've got me all wrong."

I took a small, dramatic sip from my cup of tea. "I do?" I answered. "Then let's you and me give your personal cocksucker a call, say you and your six inches'll be over in, what, say an hour? What's his name, by the way—Bill? Bob? Brett? Or is it Raheem?"

He looked up at me, his lower jaw tense. His eyes wild and flat.

"You don't know anything, Richie. You think you do, but you don't. You really don't. What a pity."

At this unsolicited judgment I began to yell, "I don't know *any*thing? *Really*? You telling me what I know or don't know? I graduated from Princeton, Mister. Or did you forget that, too?"

He smiled to himself and traced a finger along the curve of his upturned, sensual lips. He searched the walls. "I get it now. We're on *Candid Camera*, right? Where's Allen Funt?"

I hurled my ceramic cup against the wall. "Get the fuck out, you bastard! You *and* your filthy dick, just get the *fuck* out!"

Just then, at my outburst, all the circulating air rose to the ceiling and hovered there momentarily. I could not catch my breath and thought I would suffocate. David sat with his elbows on the table and his hands gnarled before his still ridiculously sensual mouth. His eyes were clenched shut and I saw the quaking of his short eyelashes, and the eyelid muscle flinching, like a small fist opening and closing. I wanted to rise with the air in the room and just flee then, and not stop at the ceiling, but to break completely free through the plaster and sheet rock and to evaporate like body sweat, or rain after it falls.

I looked at the slice of toast uneaten on its saucer. To regain a sense of normalcy, I picked up the bread and briefly nibbled at it. But it was too large a slice, or else, like the mythical Lilliputians I had read about as a boy, I was too small, and therefore I couldn't finish it.

The chairs we sat in, a gift from my mother, had swivel bottoms and I lay back and turned from side to side contemplating this new thing happening to us, to me. At last, when I looked up from my lap I saw a large, butterfly-shaped stain on the wall where the cup I had thrown had shattered. The excess liquid formed a long, straight tail that dripped into a shallow pool to the baseboard. I did not know what it meant, if anything; I only imagined the anthropomorphic shape coming to life and attacking me. I stared at it until my temples hurt and the veins in my neck throbbed with the giddy anticipation of something transfiguring about to happen to my life—no, to *our* life.

Finally, I spoke: "David, you don't know that you've ruined me. You just don't know *that!*"

And then I watched David place his hands to his ears and spin round and round in his swivel-bottomed chair. When he stopped he sat hunched over, his eyes boring into me as if he knew secrets about me I did not yet know myself, infidelities I would commit with future lovers perhaps, or contradictions in my usually rigid and self-certain morality. It was unnerving how specific the knowledge in his eyes projected: dates, names, places, sexual positions. He knew everything there was to be known about me, everything, and, at the same time, he knew nothing really. Still, he just sat there, silent and humble, lasering into me, so that his short spine curved, like his penis curved when blood and desire engorged it, and cast a shocking, prehistoric shadow upon the glossy floor tile. This was years ago now, and yet I still remember that look. And though I have tried, I have not been able to forget that look.

Lasius Niger (The Black Ant)

HE LAY IN A POOL OF ICY SWEAT, his head and chest throbbing. For a moment Peter did not know where he was. His first impulse was to scream for help, but the moment his mouth opened, and his heavy tongue lolled forward, his true identity drifted back and reentered his body. He rose heavily, slipped into his flip flops and terry robe, and walked into the darkness of his living room. He lit a votive candle and sat watching the tear-shaped flame waver under his breath. Like a fugitive ghost unable to bridge dimensions, he eyed but could not bring himself to touch the telephone perched invitingly on the arm of his sofa. "Ring me, now," Quinton had said. "I don't give a fuck if it's three o'clock in the goddamn morning, motherfucka! If you need me, call me. You bet your sweet ass I'm gonna call you."

Peter picked up the Rolex watch he had purchased with his final paycheck from *The Young and the Restless* and strapped it onto his wrist.

It was 4:32 a.m. "Too late to call now," he thought. He began to pace along the parameters of his living room, feeling the fibrous threads of terry cloth snag on the coarse hair between his buttocks. This vaguely excited him, and he lifted his knees high as he paced the room, prancing about like a bad actor in an all-male skin flick. He felt his scrotum, balloon-like, swell and lift away from his thighs. If he masturbated he might fall asleep, but he felt no desire. This wasn't the time for that.

Maybe he should read.

Just then he heard the candle sputter. When he turned, he saw the large, slick, writhing body of a black ant curling in on itself in the hot wax. The creature lay on its back, its six spindly legs collapsed across a shockingly striated underbelly. Half the exoskeleton lay in the candle's orange-blue flame, the other half—the thorax and part of the abdomen—lay submerged in the warm, viscous liquid, steadily sinking. Again, Peter felt as if he had gravitated beyond his muscular heart, his arteries, his lungs. All of a sudden he reached through the flaps of his bathrobe and grabbed hold of his erect penis. "If only I could get to sleep," he hissed. Then, from the candle, more sputtering. He wondered: *At what moment did actual death occur—at the realization that all was lost? Or maybe in the throes of a final, humiliatingly spasmodic resistance? Perhaps there was no death in the Western sense, but, instead, as the Buddhists would say, a simple 'awakening to enlightenment.'* All at once Peter ejaculated in a gush across his dining room table. "Goddamn you!" he cried. "Motherfucker, shit-eating bastard, omniscient whore! Oh yeah, oh yeah, oh yeah! Amen to that!"

A moment later the telephone rang.

Peter took up the ends of his bathrobe and quickly cleaned the sperm from between his fingers, feeling light-headed. Various objects in the room seemed to be teetering on the verge of falling: his CD player, a stuffed Snoopy doll, the King James Bible. He wiped his damp forehead with the back of his hand.

"Hello?"

Quinton's voice startled him. He glanced at his wristwatch. It was nearly five o'clock.

"I can't sleep, motherfucka," Quinton said. "Can you believe this shit? A whole pint of JB and I've woken up every hour on the goddamn hour since God knows when. How you doin'?"

It had not surprised Peter how close he and Quinton had become following Lucius' death. None of them were kids any longer; they could not afford false jealousies now. Everyone in his and Lucius' circle of friends in those days, at some point during their overlapping histories, had slept with everyone else—or, if not, had wanted to. Each man had uncovered for himself that it was not the body which had drawn them all together. On the contrary, sex had simply been a subterfuge for their various entanglements. It was as if the voice of the body was the only voice through which each man felt he could express himself and not have that expression thoroughly misconstrued. To swallow another man's penis, to penetrate him, and in turn yourself be penetrated, was a language unto itself, and had also provided each of them with a common repertoire of, say, musical notes to be sung throughout their lives, when previously, as boys, there had seemed to be only a crippling, numbing silence.

Peter gripped the phone to his breast, as Quinton, his voice dipping and screeching, sang to him.

He remembered that whenever he and Lucius had made love, he had had, on some nights more than others, a clear idea that the world, at its core, was comprised of nothing but similar voices, and that each stroke from Lucius's cock or tongue, because of the clarity and the exactitude of this language, its meticulous urgency, inspired in these voices a new song more textured and rich than the previous. With a great deal of weariness and unvented rage, Peter reflected on how his friends, himself included, had awakened to find themselves reluctant soldiers in what amounted to a virtual civil war with those who considered their language an aberrant mode of communication, one rightly deserving, as Paul says to the Romans, to be silenced by death.

A chill blew through Peter's body and he pulled his robe close about him and took a seat on the sofa. He tried to calm Quinton, who was convinced that the metallic taste at the back of his tongue was 'thrush,' an HIV-related symptom. Peter switched the receiver to his other ear.

"You're tired, Quint. You need more sleep and then you'll be fine. We can't do anything till the morning anyway."

There was a long pause.

"Quinton, you there?"

Peter heard a cough on the other end of the line.

"Goddamn. This waiting is a bitch."

"Now you know how I feel," said Peter. "All we actors do is sit around and wait. We get paid for waiting."

"Well, nobody's payin' me a red cent. Shit, I'm losin' money. You hear what I'm sayin'?"

"You want me to sing to you?"

"What, you've written lyrics to the 'Death March' now?"

"Stop that."

Quinton started once more to cry. "Wake up, baby! I'm preparing myself for the inevitable. Lucius was my nigga. His dick was up my ass and vice-versa. You gave that shit up, 'member?"

Peter swung his legs up onto the coffee table. He adjusted a seat cushion behind his back, in amused preparation for the drunken tirade he knew would follow. It always did.

"Right, Quint. I left Lucius to be a big-time Hollywood star. Only problem was they had already heard of Denzel Washington."

"You got that straight. He loved you but you had a bug up your ass, jack. Bright lights, big-city waterbug!"

"What else, Quint?"

"What else? I'll tell your ass what else, jive motherfucka. You sittin' down?"

Peter yawned, and a slight smile fell across his face. He inclined his head toward the window and noticed the sun just beginning its morning ascent. Peter only half-listened to the now mythic story of his return from Los Angeles two years ago, just before Lucius was diagnosed. He had come back with his hair in a limp jheri-curl and tossed off phrases like: "Surely you jest" and "But of course."

"What a pretentious little homo erectus I thought you were! I told Lucius that he should consider his ass lucky to have you off his hands. 'Lucky Lucius,' I called that motherfucka. Please! And what was that other shit you used to say? Oh, yeah." (Quinton was laughing now.) "'That's wild, man.' I thought I'd fucking vomit!"

There was now only the hum of breathing on Quinton's end of the phone. Peter said: "Do you believe in God, Quint? I mean, the bastard with the stream of white hair? And what about the ascension? Do you think that really happened?"

Quinton shrieked. "Hell no! Man, I put stock in what I can see with my eyes and touch with my black hands. That hocus pocus religious shit can't beat my meat. Get outta here with that crap."

Peter glanced at the hard bundle of shriveled exoskeleton turning over in the flame. From high school he remembered that male ants in particular live only long enough to mate with the queen of the nest and then soon afterwards are either killed or go off on their own and willfully die, their life's purpose fulfilled. Lucius sometimes mentioned, only half-kidding, that his own mission in life was to rid the planet of shoes with tassels, and of course white men. Peter smiled and searched the air, as if for proof of his former lover's gloriously unrepentant soul drifting in a mist toward the ceiling. He shrugged the tense feeling from his shoulders.

"I hear you, Quint. But who knows what's out there, right? You could be wrong, I mean. We all could."

Quinton cleared his throat. The timbre of his voice attempted to rise in pitch yet remained resolute, flat, disembodied.

"Most days," he said, "life pisses me off. But I tell you something, I ain't ready to turn in my gold card yet. We get our test results in the morning, right? Let's just see then. God or no fucking God, I lean on you, you lean on me. That's how us black faggots have always done it. Goddamn it."

Quinton yawned.

"Get some sleep," Peter said, not bothering to remind him that was how white faggots had always done it as well.

"Shit, I need to."

"Try."

"You bet."

Peter placed the receiver back in its cradle. He looked out the window; the sun was pink in the sky. He could feel in the crusted edges of his terry bathrobe the semen that had now dried into the fabric. He whispered to himself the first names of all his friends who had gone down in battle since his return to New York: Lucius, Reginald, Michael, Allen, Rob, Sam, Redvers, Joe, Richard, David, Carlos, Keith, Eugene, Mark—

He sat listening to the wind blow through the fallen leaves in the courtyard below his window. Suddenly, Peter could picture his body and the bodies of all his heroic comrades wafting in the breeze like so many sheets of discarded paper. He dropped instinctively to his knees. But for the first time since he had learned to recite the Lord's Prayer as a boy, the words deserted him. "Quint's right," he whispered. "The motherfucka can't really exist. And if He does, then the *hell* with His ass."

You Get What You Pay For

As one can well imagine, in my line of work I often get the opportunity to meet new and interesting people. I'm a sex surrogate for couples who want to spice up their relationships, or who are simply having trouble with intimacy. Not a legal surrogate, mind you, which requires certification, but a surrogate nonetheless. It's a good living. I have been in the business going on two years, not long by most standards, and I must confess there *are* times I'd rather be out enjoying a good jog. But mostly I wouldn't trade my profession for all the tea in China. The sense of accomplishment I feel is unequaled when a couple with whom I've worked has been able to take their relationship to a new level. Certainly too I've had my share of failures: men who wig out the moment they see their wives or girlfriends in bed with another man—especially a black man—or else other men, white men mostly, who are just a little *too* turned on by the idea of what they imagine to be my BBC; too, some women, a small percentage to be sure, almost lapse into a seizure the first time their male partner engages in fellatio, though paradoxically a desire for just this type of sexual variation is the primary reason most people contact me in the first place, whether at their own suggestion or their mate's.

Occasionally a male couple will seek out my services, which isn't anything I'm averse to. The mechanics aren't as different as some people might imagine. Usually one or both partners is going through a prolonged period of either physical or emotional frigidity—for example, showing little interest in initiating or welcoming foreplay, to cite one of the most common problem areas. It would surprise people how many lovers simply have no conception of a lead-in, that most want to hurry to the main event, as it were, as quickly as possible and get to sleep. This type of thing occurs more frequently with men rather than women—both gay and straight—and in a large measure, luckily, is quite correctable.

Take, for example, the couple with whom I've most recently worked: Willie and Marvin.

Willie—the man to whom I was closest—is the owner of a successful chain of women's shoe stores scattered throughout three of the five boroughs of New York: Manhattan, Brooklyn, and Queens. When he isn't attending to administrative duties, he spends the day caressing the soles and arches of slender, delicate feet, and engaging in small, polite chatter with his customers that often borders on the erotic. At forty-five, Willie is an attractive black man, with close-cropped, salt-and-pepper hair and a sandy complexion. In fact, he is the type to whom people find themselves instantly drawn. Willie is a natural charmer. It's part and parcel of his character, like a two-inch heel on a dress pump.

On the other hand, his partner Marvin works in a thriving investment firm on Water Street, near Wall, in downtown Manhattan. And though ten years younger, Marvin behaves, when he's home, says Willie, as if he's a man in his late fifties. To make matters worse, he spends most of his day in an office without windows, trading stocks he can never actually touch with his hands, and speaking to individuals his age or younger over the telephone whom he will never meet: who will remain, no matter how long he may do business with them, voices without distinguishing bodies or facial features, but names only: Javier, Kyle, Cynthia, Gunther. By the time he arrives home in the evening, Marvin isn't particularly in the mood for the dulcet, southern tones of his life-partner's voice. Whenever Willie tries to coax him out of his doldrums—by placing a Wyndham Hill CD on the stereo, and suggesting a sensual massage to go with it, Marvin responds with agitation. "Niggah, *please!*" he says, and storms into another room. Sometimes he leaves altogether, and goes to a bar in Greenwich Village, whereupon he drinks and flirts with men who don't know enough about themselves, or Marvin, for that matter, to really diffuse his frustration. After a few hours he returns, inebriated and smelling of Pall Malls and a heady mixture of cheap colognes. By this time Willie has lost his own calm: he's cleaned their apartment from top to bottom, at least once, and telephoned several mutual friends, seeking advice. It was one of these friends—a woman by the name of Miranda—who suggested to Willie that he and Marvin seek out my services.

I've known Miranda longer than any of my clients. In fact, she's the reason I got into the business. After my arrival in New York I drifted about from one ad agency to another, not quite sure of my focus or even my ambition. At one particular agency I struck up a friendship with Miranda, who at the time was Senior Manager of her firm's domestic automobile accounts. During lunch we'd walk through Central Park, swapping random, personal anecdotes, like what our mothers' maiden names were, and how old we'd been the first time that someone special had French-kissed us. One afternoon, while seated on a park bench near the Reservoir, I confessed to Miranda my attraction to her. At the time we were eating frozen ices—me tangerine, she chocolate—and watching some owner's unleashed terrier stalk a flock of unsuspecting pigeons. Without skipping a beat, Miranda spread the fingers of her left hand. "I'm a married woman," she said. I nodded: "I know." A few moments later, she spoke of herself and her husband, Holden, a robust, hirsute construction engineer, who enjoyed being anally penetrated, but who otherwise she assured me was neither homosexual nor bisexual by any conventional definition. She looked at me. "Would you be interested? We'll pay you. You can say no." By day's end I walked into Miranda's office and invited myself to dinner. That was eighteen months ago.

As far as Willie and Marvin are concerned, it wasn't clear in the beginning, to either them or me, in what way having a sex surrogate would improve their relationship. The three of us had dinner one evening, at Cinco de Mayo, a Mexican restaurant near where I live on Broome Street, in Soho. Willie was the more talkative of the two. Marvin fussed with his dinner napkin for most of the evening, only piping up near the end to ask if I was both active and passive when it came to anal intercourse; he phrased his question, however, in much cruder terms. I answered that he need not worry in that area, that I was quite versatile and had few inhibitions. This response seemed to please him, as he neatly folded his napkin and dropped it onto his plate. Next, he signaled our waiter and proceeded to order for each of us three large frozen margaritas.

A second meeting was quickly arranged to discuss health concerns, such as each man's HIV status, his history of venereal diseases, mental illness, and any other health issue we should all be briefed on before deciding to proceed or not. (The end result was that we were all, amazing to me, HIV negative.) At our third meeting—which the three of us had agreed to refer to as our first official session—I arrived dressed in a United Parcel Service worker's uniform: brown shirt and trousers. Willie opened the door and began to immediately enact the role that had been mutually decided on. At that point, Marvin had not yet arrived. According to the script we three had co-authored, Willie and I were to be already in the throes of things when Marvin was to walk in and catch us. For a moment, we were to feign surprise and panic, Willie and I. Then, to diffuse a potentially explosive situation, as the outside party I was to then make a graceful motion to integrate Marvin into his role. Reluctant at first, Marvin was scripted to ultimately give in and take an active part in our little scenario—"active," for him, being the operative word. Eventually, my own role was to diminish the longer the scene was played out, until finally I was to become simply an observer. In fact, I was to take photographs, which the three of us would then, at a later date, sit down to evaluate.

Things went well between us for the first half-dozen sessions—in which I was variously, as I've stated already, a UPS delivery man, the superintendent of their co-op, a member of the Jehovah's Witnesses (that was new and different), a next door neighbor, a co-worker from Marvin's firm, and a NYNEX telephone repairman. After a while, however, I began to notice that the longer the sessions lasted—in actual hours, that is—the more difficult I found it to disengage myself and to simply take pictures. I realized that I genuinely liked my newest clients (Prior to these two, I had never been contracted by a couple in which both were of African descent—one or the other, sure, but not the pair; maybe this was the common ground between us. Who's to say?). And though the youngest was ten years older than I was, at twenty-six, and his partner ten years older than that, I nonetheless felt a tremendous sense of kinship with them both.

When I told Miranda about it, after one of *our* sessions, I thought she'd laugh in my face and say: I told you so. You made your bed, now lie in it. But her response threw me. Willie and Marvin had also been to see her to discuss the growing intimacy developing among the three of us.

"What did they say?" I wanted to know.

"I'm no tattletale," said Miranda. "But you went to college. Figure it out. What else: they're smitten with you, baby."

Miranda tossed her curly red mane over a shoulder and fixed me with those liquid brown eyes of hers.

"Face it," she said, drawing a peach-colored sheet up to her nude midsection, but leaving her perfectly rounded breasts exposed. "Those two haven't done this sort of thing before. They're as straight as they come for gay men. Okay? Especially that Marvin: he couldn't screw a side of beef unless it had been stamped USDA Approved. All this is a bit overwhelming to them, and a great big freaking high, to boot. The problem: How to keep a professional distance and enjoy yourself at the same time. Both for them and…(here she paused for dramatic effect)… for you."

Miranda laced her fingers business-like in her lap.

"Holden and I are different," she said. "You weren't our first surrogate. As we told you during our interview, we'd tried two other men before we found you. Those other jerks were capitalist morons, in it for the money and the giddy pleasure of having an orifice to stick their miserable joysticks in—man or woman didn't matter. One of them called Holden a fag and I chased the fucker out of our apartment so fast he almost forgot his condoms. A graduate of Harvard, or so he said; but crude, rude, and lewd. You were a whole new breed. Holden recognized it the first time we had dinner. Me, I'd already made my decision after you told me you'd read Maupassant's *Une Vie*. I said to myself: He's bright, articulate, dresses like he means it. *And* speaks French, on top of it. Why the hell not?"

Just then Holden came out of the bathroom, with a blue and white striped beach towel wrapped about his thick waist. He was rugged-looking, with jet black hair and a Van Dyke. On his left pectoral was a tattoo of a mermaid with a green tail and red hair; Miranda's name was written, in blue ink, underneath the tailfin.

"You're too good at your work, Clay," he sighed, plopping himself next to his wife, on the bed. "People who aren't experienced at this sort of thing have no sense of the boundaries involved."

"Look who's talking, Romeo," Miranda chimed in. She ran her fingers goodnaturedly through Holden's freshly showered hair, then turned to address me.

"Much to his own surprise, *and mine*, this one here's found himself quite attached to you, *Monsieur* Brown Bomber."

"'Brown' what?"

"The Brown Bomber, hon'. Holden's nickname for you. What, you didn't know about it? It's after some boxer, isn't it?"

Holden picked up a bottle of Aloe Vera lotion and squeezed a small amount onto his hands. "Randy, please," he said, rubbing the lotion onto his hairy arms and chest. "You're embarrassing us both, for chrissakes."

Although Miranda addressed the following words to me, she nonetheless continued to face her husband, who continued to rub more lotion onto his legs and buttocks.

"I'm not embarrassing Clay. Am I, Clay? It's you I'm embarrassing. Isn't that right, sweetie? Clay's just tickled pink to know he's the object of so many people's affections. You'd be the same in his shoes. I would too. Hell, who wouldn't? But the bottom line is—" Here, Miranda reached for the brocaded purse I'd given her as a gift on her last birthday, which was on the nighttable, and withdrew a slender brown cigarette; the tone of her voice had changed: it was less musical, characterized now by a scratchy distortion—"the bottom line is," she said, striking a match to her cigarette and lighting it, "these relationships can't go on forever."

She caught my eye.

"I'm talking about the three of us, Clay: you, me, Holden. The same applies—don't think for a minute it doesn't—to what's presently brewing between yourself and your other clientele, especially you-know-who. Things have a natural shelf-life—well, if not exactly 'natural,' then a shelf-life that's built into the core of the relationship itself. This is true whether it's a marriage, like mine and Holden's, or simply a hired gun— like you are to us, if you get my meaning."

Miranda looked from her husband's face to mine.

"Surely you two boys know what I'm talking about?"

Neither Holden nor I responded.

"Don't tell me, let me guess." She tossed her hair over a pale shoulder. "I'm the only one who's even considered just when we'd have to dissolve this little arrangement of ours. Am I close?"

Holden stood up from the bed.

"Randy, please."

"*Score!*"

"I thought things were working out fine between the three of us. You mean to say, it wasn't?"

"What do you think? Fine for you, or fine for me? There's a difference, you know."

Eyeing my briefs on the floor, I made a move to reach them.

"And where do you think *you're* going, *Monsieur* Brown?" asked Miranda.

"I should leave," I said. "After all, this is between you and Holden. I'm in the way here."

Miranda took a drag of her cigarette. "No way, José," she said. "You've been fucking my husband for months. I'd say that puts you right, smack, dab in the middle. Wouldn't you say so, hon'?"

She dropped the peach-colored sheet from her waist. Her breasts bounced as she crawled over the bed to stand next to Holden.

"You think Clay's a member of the family now?" she prodded.

Her husband remained silent.

"He's a high-priced whore; that's what he is. We pay him; he delivers the goods. It's as uncomplicated as that. Holden, you're *my* husband. I married you, not him. For fuck's sake! We can't adopt the man. For one thing he's black. How would that look?"

Here, she paused and glanced over at me. Already I had one foot stuck through a leg of my briefs.

"Or is that what you both planned?" Her whole body shook with suspicion. "Somebody answer me, goddamn it. *Now!*"

Holden went to comfort his wife, who, in a matter of a few moments, had gone from utter calm to a kind of frenzied, moral uncertainty.

At this point, I dressed hurriedly and saw myself to the door of their apartment. Before I left, I heard Miranda's anguished voice call out to me: "It's up to you, Clay! You've got to be the one to make the break. Because they won't. And you know exactly who I mean, Clay. Don't play dumb!"

On some gut level I knew that Miranda was right. In a mere six weeks, the three of us had gotten awfully close, very quickly—Willie, Marvin, and I; just as Miranda, Holden, and I had struck up a similarly strong bond, though over a far longer period. And my time with Willie and Marvin, for some reason, had increasingly filled what I hadn't realized was a void in my life. The woman with whom I was involved had become, during this time, disenchanted with the long hours I devoted to my work— not that she took exception to my having sex with other men; interestingly enough, it was other women she felt most threatened by. When I tried to explain the professional borders I worked within—borders, however, I found expanding more and more—she moved out of our apartment and into the eastside condo of a girlfriend who, also a fashion model, was presently out of the country.

Willie and Marvin, of course, like most of my clients—Miranda and Holden notwithstanding—knew nothing of my relationships outside of them. I had made it a policy to keep my private affairs separate from my professional engagements, and for nearly two years of being a surrogate it had worked. But one afternoon while arranging a session with Willie over the phone, I let it slip that I was feeling particularly off-balance these days since my fiancée had left me. It was clients like Marvin and himself, I said, who helped take the edge off my bruised ego. Willie was sympathetic, not that I expected otherwise, and before hanging up he suggested I stop by the apartment that evening for dinner—not one of our usual sessions, he added, just a quiet evening among "friends"—this being how he put it. And since I was feeling so despondent, I agreed. But immediately after answering yes, I could have kicked myself for my weak-willed and needy character.

I reached the Seventh Avenue subway stop, in Park Slope, at 7 p.m. Unlike previous occasions, I arrived dressed in my own clothes rather than wearing a costume of one sort or another, which is how we had agreed to conduct each of our formal sessions. (During the interview process, Marvin had admitted to being more easily aroused if his imagination were stimulated by some outside agent, preferably something he'd fantasized about, and to which he had already formed an erotic connection.) Instead, that evening I dressed in a pair of loose-fitting, beige chinos, and, as it was still warm out for October, a lightweight sweater and denim jacket. This time Marvin met me at the door, and I was for a moment taken aback by his warm greeting; usually it took him a good hour to relax enough to even participate fully in our sessions.

"How're you, Clay?" he asked, taking out of my hands the bottle of wine I'd brought with me.

"I suppose Willie's told you my troubles," I said.

Marvin nodded, and led me further inside the apartment.

"All these weeks," he said, "and I've not asked you about *your* life, who's got you by the balls, etcetera. Sometimes I'm so self-absorbed."

He took me by the elbow. "But you're okay, now?"

"As well as can be expected," I shrugged. "Glad I'm here."

"We are, too. Aren't we, baby?" said Marvin, throwing his voice in the direction of the kitchen.

"Glad you could make it," shouted Willie, from the other room.

"Thanks for inviting me," I answered.

Marvin ordered me to sit and disappeared himself into the kitchen with Willie. I could hear their two voices rising and falling in hushed, affectionate cadences to one another, and once again I felt, as I often had, the warm satisfaction of a job well-done.

When next Marvin entered the sitting room, Willie followed behind him.

"Clay," he said, moving toward me with his hand outstretched, which I attempted to shake. But Willie would have none of my formality, and pulled me towards him, in an embrace. "Welcome, sir, into our humble home."

"Oh, Willie," I said. "Thank you. Thank you both."

That evening I told the two of them the story of my life. It isn't the sort of story most people would imagine a person like me, who does the type of work I do, would tell. There isn't anything remarkable about the way I've lived, or about the various people I've known. In many ways my story is a rather bland one, and except for a couple of events I would either embellish or else downplay (to show myself in a poor or flattering light, depending upon the desired effect), both Willie and Marvin for the most part listened with respectful anticipation to every word. Several times Willie had to leave the room to see to the trio of Cornish hens he was preparing out in the kitchen, whereupon Marvin took the initiative to refill each of our glasses with more of the Chardonnay I had brought. When Willie returned, I would resume my narrative, pausing here and there, at their urging, to clarify a particular episode I hadn't explained fully, and keeping all digressions to an absolute minimum. Throughout, my eyes would light on their two strong, compassionate faces, and I felt my connection to them all the more true and right, in spite of Miranda's warning.

I had moved to the city directly after graduating from college, I said, to put as great a distance between my overbearing parents and siblings as possible. Of my two brothers and one sister I was the youngest, and the only one of us not interested in pursuing a traditional life-course. In college, I had studied French literature and philosophy, and in the words of my father, doing so I had made it virtually a certainty that I was not trained to do anything thought useful in the society in which I lived. Too, I had sung in one of the several all-male glee clubs at my alma mater, the Mighty Gents. And to top it off, my junior year I'd written and starred in a one-man performance piece, in which I stood naked on stage for forty-five minutes and recited fragments from my personal journal, interspersed with minstrel songs depicting the blatant racism of the early 1900s. After that, I told them, I had no trouble getting a date for the rest of my college career, especially with white students—to which we all laughed in knowing commiseration, and then moved into the dining room.

During dinner, we each explained to the others how we had come to know our sexual selves.

Growing up in Charleston, South Carolina, Willie said he'd always known he was more attracted to little boys than little girls.

"Man, I was sweet on lil' Jimmie Taylor 'fore I knew what a Tonka truck *was*! And did I care? Not one bit! Jimmie just had to holler, and I was over that fence faster than you could shake a stick at a garter snake!" For his part, Marvin had come into his erotic knowledge quite late.

"When the other guys were out chasing skirts," he said, taking up one of the bread rolls Willie had heated, and spreading butter on it, "I was up in my room doing sums. You know, trying to prove that two plus two didn't always equal four, that there had to be other values in between that figure. See, with my family's income, I knew intuitively that a ten dollar bill didn't always buy the same merchandise week after week; that the price of things fluctuated, depending on which of my brothers needed shoes that week, or how much overtime my old man put in on the job. And this wasn't the case just with money, but with everything: people, history, relationships. You pay for what you get, not the other way 'round. And not a damn thing was fixed in stone. Nothing."

At my turn, I said, modestly, that I'd been attracted to both men and to women for as long as I could remember. That it had never been a matter of *choosing* between the two for me. I confessed that I had never felt what some people did: torn down the middle; that when they were involved with a man, they were simultaneously longing in their hearts and loins for a woman. That didn't describe my experiences. My lovers hadn't all been predisposed the same way I was, I said, to bisexuality—and therein lay the rub. In the past, I simply got around the issue by being as forthright and honest in my feelings as I could in a given situation.

"It's worked for me just fine," I said, stuffing a forkful of string beans into my mouth, to keep from breaking. "That is, until now."

After dinner, Willie ushered me into the living room, and Marvin stayed behind to prepare a pot of European coffee. While Marvin was in the kitchen, Willie took the opportunity to tell me the story of how the two of them had met. Marvin had come into one of Willie's shoe stores with his then-wife, Roni, a pretty woman who was half-Filipino and half-black. As Willie attended to Roni—bringing out stack after stack of size six slingback pumps—the three struck up a conversation, in which it was discovered that Willie, like Roni, had attended Howard University, which claimed a veritable Who's Who's list of famous black Americans. " 'Not that either of us are exactly famous,' said Roni, laughing, but added: 'A person can never know, can they?' At this, she parted her pretty lips and began to warble, in a truly pitiful soprano, the opening verse to *La Mort de l'Amour*, an aria which the opera singer Jessye Norman, a graduate of Howard, had once recorded."

At this point, Marvin entered the conversation, placing our cups of espresso on the low coffee table.

"You telling that old story again?" he asked, shaking his head.

Willie was clearly in a good mood. It was such a joy for me to see the both of them so happy.

"And what if I am, Negro?" he asked, picking up one of the small, white cups ringed in China blue along the rim off the table and bringing it to his lips. "Who 'gon stop me? You and *whose* army?"

Marvin threw up his hands, playfully. "My name's Bennett," he said, "and I ain't in it," after which he hitched up his trousers at the knee and sat down next to me. He was smiling too. "All's I'm saying, man, is I wouldn't stir up no dead bones, if I was you. Might see a ghost, and then where'd we be? Shit! That's all I need *tonight!*"

Willie laughed, and turned to face me. "Roni's a friend of ours," he said, by way of an explanation. "She's married to some other fellow now. Lives in Atlanta. Got a baby daughter she named after Marvin's mother. A wonderful woman. Treats me just like family. God bless her."

Conversation quieted, as each man took up his cup and sipped from it. I looked about the room at the life my newest "friends" had made with one another, over the eight years they'd been a couple. I tried to picture the battles they'd had to face over that time, some won, others lost. Willie leaned back in his cushioned chair and sighed contentedly; Marvin, I noticed, had gotten up to flip through his extensive music collection. Feeling somewhat idle, albeit pleasantly, on the far wall, near the upright bookcase, I saw a reproduction of a painting by William H. Johnson, entitled "Young Man in a Vest." It was a painting I'd of course seen before, on my numerous visits, but which now—because of Marvin's comment—drew my attention in a new and pointed way. The young man stared out from the frame as though hovering, ghost-like, in mid-air, as if he wanted to speak, or was already speaking, but because he was a painting he couldn't be heard. Dressed in a dark suit, vest, and necktie, the young man in the painting looked to be about my age, but wiser. After all, he would not have found himself in my situation—in the middle, betwixt two pairs of longtime loves, one of whom had called me a whore. He'd have backed out before now. Only I was the fool.

That night, after we three had made love, I awoke from a dream in which I had killed my mother and had had sex with my father. Unnerved by these images, I slipped off before morning and returned to my own apartment. Later that afternoon I telephoned Willie and thanked him for the lovely evening I'd had, and for the good food; I hated myself for lying, but I didn't dare confess to him the truth: that I feared becoming a parasite in his and Marvin's life, just as I had become one in Miranda and Holden's. I apologized too for leaving the way I did—abruptly and without saying goodbye. But I was just so darn happy, I said. I was afraid I'd simply explode and make a mess, thereby waking up the two of them from what looked to be a sound sleep. But the fact of the matter—which I couldn't tell to anyone—was that Miranda was partly right: As a sex surrogate I was of use to other couples just as long as I provided a service that helped one or both partners overcome an impediment to their sexual enjoyment. Beyond that I was useless. Such a person might even do more harm than good were he to exceed his primary function, or stay around longer than was necessary, no matter how well the separate parties enjoyed one another's company.

I was at a crisis. The first I'd had, or admitted to having, since I'd decided to leave Rochester and move to New York City. For me, it wasn't a matter of whether to be involved with men or women—it was never that; I was simply afraid of being involved with anyone, for fear of being responsible to them, of giving up something I felt I couldn't afford to give up. It was the reason I'd literally jumped at Miranda and Holden's offer to be their boy-toy. Between the two of them, I could have my cake and eat it too. Why not? To admit to such a thing was a huge step for me. Immediately I phoned up my fiancee, Brenda, and told her about my dream of killing my mother and about having sex with my father, and what I believed was its significance. She was in the middle of preparing dinner when I called. She said, "Oh, Clay. You should see someone about that. Really, you should. But, look, honey, can I phone you back tomorrow? I've a friend over for dinner—and, well, you know how it is."

"Sure, Brenda," I said. "No problem."

When I saw Brenda the following week—at Cinco de Mayo, our favorite restaurant—she opened up her purse and returned to me her engagement ring.

"Forgive me," she said, glancing away. She had recently begun to grow her hair back out, and was using a brighter shade of lipgloss which I liked.

"What is this, Brenda? What are you doing?"

"I've made a decision, Clay," she said. "I can't marry you. I'm sorry."

"I don't understand. What do you mean, you can't marry me? But you've already said yes."

"I know I have, Clay."

I tried slipping the ring back onto Brenda's finger, but she crossed her arms over her chest to prevent me.

"You know? Then how can you say what you're saying? How can anybody do that?"

She was tearing now. I dropped the ring on the table and pushed it over to her.

"You take this," I said. "Go on. Take it."

Finally, Brenda said: "You didn't have to ask me, Clay. I was happy the way things were. True, I went along with it. So I'm to blame too. But you...you shouldn't have asked me if you didn't mean it. But you did, Clay. How could you mean it? It's not in you to mean it."

Discreetly, Brenda removed a designer handkerchief from her handbag and blew her nose.

"Maybe as a couple we gave one another too much rope," she said. "And we hanged ourselves with it. Maybe people who love one another aren't supposed to have that much freedom. And I took all those photo shoots. To countries I'd never been to but all my life have dreamed of visiting. I didn't want to deny myself, Clay. That was my mother's ball and chain. Maybe if I'd stayed home more often. Or you had. That's why I didn't mind your work at first. I figured we were special people. We were big people, whereas everyone around us was small. Small and frightened. But not us."

Brenda began to fold the handkerchief in a way I'd seen Marvin do when he was agitated—in halves, then in quarters.

"You won't take back the ring?"

She shook her head. "No."

"Fine. I'll return it and get back my $3,000."

"Whatever you want, Clay."

I looked at her. "Whatever I want?"

"Yes."

"I asked you to be my wife. That's what I wanted."

"I know you did."

"And now you're saying you can't?"

"That's right."

I picked up the ring off the table and slipped it inside my blazer pocket.

"Then *fuck* you," I said. "Fuck *you*."

The waiter for our station lingered off to the side. I could see him out of the corner of my eye—a tall, lemon-faced man with shiny black hair—waiting for us to lift up the menus, and make a decision.

Brenda touched my wrist. I flinched.

"Just let it go, Clay," she said. "Please."

"Let what go? I'm perfectly fine, thank-you."

"This pretending to be what you're not. You aren't angry at me. How could you be? At whom are you angry, Clay? Tell me. I'm listening."

I picked up the sleek menu and opened it. "What do you care to eat, *Mademoiselle*? They're waiting."

"We used to talk all the time, Clay. But we haven't spoken in months. Here's our chance. Come on, speak to me."

"This is crazy."

"Maybe. Maybe not. We won't know unless we try."

I put down the menu and took hold of Brenda's hand.

"Tell me what it is you *need*?" I said. "I'll give it to you. I promise I will. Just don't leave me. Don't. I couldn't take that."

"Oh, Clay!" Brenda snatched back the hand I was holding. "Stop talking to me as if I am one of your clients! I'm not one of them. I don't pay you for your services. Never have. When you talk to me I want to hear *your* voice, not the voice you *think* I want to hear. But the voice of the man I've known these last three years. Who used to do Jeanne Moreau impersonations at three in the morning, and who liked to have his earlobes stroked. Do you know where that person is? Do you?"

When I didn't answer, Brenda grabbed her handbag.

"I guess not." Standing up, she towered over me. "I'm leaving now, Clay. Call me if you want to talk—about your father, or anything else. But not about us. That's finished. All right?"

"Sure, Brenda," I said. "Whatever *you* want."

"Thank you, Clay. For once."

Later, when I tried to contact Miranda, to tell her about my newest woes, her husband Holden told me, over the phone, that she didn't care to speak to me either.

"Haven't you made us suffer enough?" he asked, and added, before hanging up, that I shouldn't try to contact them ever again. "We're through with all that modern, new-age, hocus pocus, self-help rigmarole," he said. "None of it works. It just tricks poor, unsuspecting people like my wife and me into *believing* that we're actually making progress in our lives, when really we're just backsliding the whole time right into Hell itself."

For the next several days, I kept a low profile. At night, my phone would ring nonstop. I'd let the answering machine click on and screened my calls; each time it was only a potential client who'd heard of my services from someone else, and who desired to meet me for an interview; or else a current client who was simply worried over my sudden disappearance, and what significance that held for him or her and their own sessions. After a couple of weeks I drafted a letter and mailed it to these people, assuring them of my eventual return. I had only taken a long-needed vacation. I wrote: "Not to worry. Life is good." Each of my clients received one of these letters except for Miranda and Holden, and of course Willie and Marvin, to whom I sent nothing. I needed them to hate me, otherwise their pity would have yoked me to them all the more. Their friendship was a complication I didn't need, nor my self-respect could afford.

One evening I saw Marvin at a bar in the Village. He was drinking tequila shots and flirting with a twenty-ish year old Latino, who in turn was himself flirting with someone on the other side of the pool table. When Marvin saw me he asked if I cared to go home with him. I declined, whereupon he promptly tossed what remained of his drink into my face and rushed out of the bar. I followed him into the street.

"I can explain," I said.

He shook my hand from his arm.

"What's there to explain? Two plus two is always four, in your book. Isn't it? What did we expect? You pay the price of the ticket you see the show. Beyond that, what else is there? *Zilch*, say the Germans. That's what."

Marvin began to walk away. I caught up to him.

"Tell Willie I'll call," I said. "I promise."

"Yeah. And I'm Porky Pig: '*Th-th-that's all folks!*'" His eyes cut me bitterly—to the quick, you might say. "And you're a *brother* too." This last word he hurled at me, as if it were a dull weapon that had long ago outlived its usefulness.

"But, Marvin—" I said, taking hold of his arm.

Because of his drunken state, he twisted about in my grip, unable to free himself.

"Let go," he cried. "We trusted you. Willie. Me. We welcomed you into our home—our *home*, man! Even our *goddamn* kitchen! Don't that mean nothing to you?"

"Come here," I said, and pulled Marvin to my chest. He smelled like he'd been drinking for days. I embraced him. Other men from inside the bar began to filter out onto the sidewalk, and pass by us on their way to other bars, or to the subway, or wherever. Some lingered, as if to eavesdrop on what Marvin and I said to one another, then shyly left. Other men turned their heads the other way, perhaps fearful of being asked to lend a hand. No one wanted to be involved. And who could blame them? Mostly, these were black men like ourselves. The few whites who ventured out of the bar showed a heightened interest, but they too merely circled the two of us, standing on the corner. We were all of us insects buzzing around a too-bright streetlamp: at once waiting for and afraid of the pitchblack darkness. Somehow I managed to flag down a taxi and deposited Marvin in the backseat. After slipping the driver a twenty dollar bill, I told him my friend's address, and closed the door. I stood on the sidewalk and watched the taxicab disappear into the ebb and flow of the Westside Highway. After that, I walked through the streets of lower Manhattan, kicking at cigarette butts and bottle caps, thinking all the while about the bad feeling in my chest, and the best way to make peace with it.

The next morning I woke up next to a woman I had picked up in a bar along West 4th Street—'Down the Hatch,' I think it was called. She had red hair and full, high-perched breasts, and when I saw her I wanted nothing more than to lose myself inside her opalescent skin. Of course, I had glimpsed in her an image of Miranda, and had believed that by embracing this woman I would be simultaneously forgiven by my former client/friend, whom I was certain by this time hated me, as Marvin hated me, and as Willie did—and Lord knew who else. After the woman awoke—her name was Jessica—I told her, quite bluntly, the kind of work I did for a living. I didn't care to have anyone getting too attached to me. In my profession, I said, a man couldn't afford to get personally attached to people outside the business, whether men or women—*both* were my clients, I stressed. Further, if a meaningful relationship was what she was after, then she had gone home with the wrong gentleman. I watched Jessica collect her things—her transparent, tie-dyed blouse, her black, Lycra unitard, and ankle-high boots—and saw her to the door, at which point she nearly broke her neck running for the elevator. When she left I fixed myself a light breakfast and sat down naked in the middle of my living room floor to eat it. I thought to myself: "Is this all there is—green eggs and ham?" I laughed out loud at the cliché I was presenting, the mentally cracked escort. Before I could stop myself, I dug my fist into my plate and smeared a handful of runny eggs all over my face and neck. I urinated down my leg. For hours I didn't budge. Day came and went. Darkness fell. It hadn't occurred to me, living the kind of protected life I'd lived—first staying with my parents, then going directly to school—that I would ever need to make it through such a night. But everything descended upon me so quickly; I hadn't time to make preparations. Before long, my body simply gave way under me. Sleep came easier than I expected. I didn't dream, or if I did I couldn't remember the details. The next day, the sun streamed in in wide, sweeping arcs through the window, and the hair beneath my arms prickled, as if each follicle was a stiff, new growth. I spent all that morning and part of the afternoon cleaning the piss stain from my expensive carpet. I took a long shower.

That evening I telephoned my parents, and after speaking several minutes with my mother, I asked her to call my father to the phone.

"Hello, Dad?" I said.

My father was silent for a long while. Then he asked: "You okay down there, boy? You don't need nothing, do you? Some money? Want your mother and me to send you something?"

"No, Dad," I said. "I was just calling. It's been too long. I wanted to hear your voice, that's all. Talk to me, a while."

Again, he quieted. I felt he wanted to ask me a question, but he didn't know how to phrase it, and so let it drop. A moment later, my mother's agitated voice came on the line.

"What did you say to your father, Claymore?"

"Nothing, Mom."

"Well, you must've said something. You tell him what you're doing down there? Did you shove *that* in his face?"

"No, Mom," I said. "I just wanted him to speak to me."

She paused; then said, "Boy, you outta your mind. Everybody's not like you. People don't think the way you think. You can't just go around forcing yourself on people. It just isn't fair. You gotta let people breathe, otherwise they shrivel up and die on you. Then all you've got is a dead body. Is that what you want? You want a whole bunch of dead bodies on your hands?"

"No, Mom. I don't."

"Then don't try people," she said.

"Yes, Mom."

After hanging up the phone, I took another shower; this one much longer. I washed my whole body several times: under my arms, the small of my back, between my thighs, and my backside. It was as if I'd never bathed; I couldn't get clean enough. Before falling asleep that night I resolved to not ever contact my natural parents again, for however long I lived. It was the best solution for them and for me. I have never really cared for my siblings, nor they for me. Ours is a family in name and blood only. The loyalty we feel towards one another, above all, is a conventional loyalty; it is therefore an easy one to pin down and duplicate, and requires no act of faith to bring it to life—no jolt of bodily passion to give it form and shape. In many ways, our family is already a dead one; I suspect my mother knows this, but is unable to face it. What remains simply is for each of us to realize this fact. Perhaps the reason I derive so much pure joy from my line of work—despite the moral strictures against it—has to do with my being on such direct terms with the perishable body. In making love to anyone, I can never afford to lose sight of the certainty that in my hands, under the brush of my tongue, even within my bowels, I hold life, as God has revealed it to us. To know such a thing, I believe, is truly humbling. Before, I had only half-sensed this dimension to love-making, whether with strangers or with people I've known and, in my way, cared for—for instance, Brenda. Or Willie and Marvin. Of course, there's Miranda, whose beauty, to quote from a poem by Apollinaire, similarly terrified me: "*Cette femme était si belle / Qu'elle me faisait peur.*" Then, I would quickly flee from having to face such knowledge, that to live, for some of us, is often little different from being dead, just as other people in my life here in this city have fled from knowing me for similar reasons. I don't want to die without knowing all there is to know in the world; by the same logic, nor—now that I'm so expert at it—do I want to die without *bodily* loving every single human being I can. It's the way I've chosen to live my life: every day I awake I put myself at risk. It's the least I can do.

The Rest of Us

IT WAS VERY WARM IN THE ROOM BECAUSE of the broken air conditioning, and because the breeze coming through the opened window had not cooled, though it was nearly 11:30 p.m. Hanging on the walls were various black and white photographs of selected parts of the human body—arms, backs, distended necks—in which the models' faces were in shadow or otherwise hidden from view. These images were all of men: dark-complexioned men with well-developed musculature and gleaming, hairless torsos. Atop the chest-of-drawers sat two playbills from a recent production at the Public Theater, and next to them a pair of silver-rimmed, antique eyeglasses, the type worn curled about the ears; in addition, an autographed copy of Rupert Kinnard's comic serial, *B.B. and the Diva*, sat propped open on the steamer trunk, beneath the window. A few feet away, two men lay next to one another, in bed—one fair, the other a shade or two darker, and in terms of physique not remotely like the models in the photographs—each having a difficult time trying to fall asleep.

One of the men, Martin, pushed back the rose-patterned, linen bedsheet, and sat up.

"I don't think you should blame me," he said. Martin had a slender build and hazel eyes, with flecks of dark coloring about the irises. As he spoke, his delicate hands beat the air like wings.

"I'm not blaming you," answered Paul, his lover. The second man did not turn around to say this, but instead kept his back facing the room.

Martin countered. "Yes, you are. Don't say you aren't doing something when it's as plain as the nose on your face that you are doing it. You're blaming me. I don't like to be blamed for what I didn't do. No one would."

"Nobody's blaming you, Marty," Paul answered, looking now over his shoulder at the other man. "All I said was that maybe it didn't show good judgment. If that's blame, then what more can I say? You won't let me say anything else. If I do, if I try, then I'm being a sonafabitch. Well, I'm not a sonafabitch. And I won't accept being called one."

"You're twisting my words," Martin said.

"Oh, I am?"

"Yes."

Paul turned completely around, so that he and Martin were facing one another.

"Fine, then. I'm twisting them. And I'm sorry. Now can we get some sleep. It'll be morning soon."

"It's 11:30 at night," Martin said, pouting all of a sudden. "It won't be morning for hours yet."

The other man, Paul, sat up in bed and yawned. He was built more stoutly than his lover, and had a shaved head. At Syracuse, Paul had played fullback on the football team; but he hadn't lifted weights in years, and now his body had softened and spread.

"Okay," he said, patting his fleshy stomach. "You win. I do apologize if I blamed you. It's just that I didn't want you hurt. I care for you. Is that so horrible?"

Martin stepped out of bed and went into the bathroom for a quick pee. He considered taking a pill for his back pain, but because the medication often caused him to awake groggy he decided against it. When he returned, Paul had sat up and was flipping the pages of a fitness magazine.

"I know why you read those," Martin said, climbing into bed. He wanted to assert himself, to make up ground for his earlier tantrum. "It's for the photos of near-naked men, and not for the poorly written articles on health and fitness. Those beefy white boys turn you on. Admit it."

Paul grimaced and threw the magazine across the room at Martin, who quickly ducked to avoid being struck by it. The two men smiled at one another. Everything was going to be okay between them. After all, they had survived worse fights.

"Those guys could have hurt us," Paul said, his voice louder than he had meant it to be. "You know? I don't want anything bad to happen to you. Tell me, what's so wrong with that?"

"What about yourself?"

"I don't want anything bad to happen to me either. Satisfied?"

Martin offered a rebuttal. "But it isn't as if I haven't done it before— laid my head on your shoulder. I've done it lots of times."

"I don't remember you doing that," said Paul, shrugging.

"Well, I have. And what about taking your arm? Or placing my hand in your lap or on your thigh? I've done that, too. What makes things so different this time?"

That Paul's voice was so loud it surprised even him. "Because we were on the subway, that's why, Marty. On a subway we wouldn't have been able to get help, or to escape were something to happen."

"But I was tired," his lover offered. "I laid my head on your shoulder because of that, not because I wasn't worried about us being attacked. I *was* worried. But I don't always think about that. Sometimes I just want to be tired, or I want to take your hand. I don't want to have to think about other people. Other people don't matter. They do, but they don't. Or they shouldn't. I'm all confused."

A small, adjustable lamp sat on a table next to the bed, spreading a faint glow of illumination against the white wall. Martin, who, like Paul, was nude, scratched himself between his lightly perspiring thighs, and then sniffed his fingers.

"It's fucking hot," he said.

"Yes," echoed Paul. "Did you call the repair people again?"

"They told me the guy would be by tonight."

Paul glanced at the clock next to the lamp on the table. It was now almost midnight.

"Maybe he'll still make it."

Martin turned to him and smiled.

"Sure," he said. "And I'm Diva Touché," referring to one of the more flamboyant characters in Rupert Kinnard's comic serial.

They both laughed, and punched one another about the arms and chest a little roughly.

After a while the two men fell silent. Paul casually picked up the fitness magazine and opened it to a photograph of a dark-haired man dressed in snug-fitting workout shorts, and no shirt, gripping a set of dumbbells in each hand—the classic heterosexual strongman pose. The man was drenched in sweat, and every muscle in his body was tensed and on display, including the slightly elongated bulge of his penis. And not a hair was out of place. From this, alone, Paul felt the stirrings of an erection. He hated himself for being so easily manipulated. Martin was right of course. The magazine was clearly marketed primarily towards gay men. However, its slick production was aimed also at straights. And as the dominant consumers, the egos of these men needed to be protected from the horrible implication that they *might* be queer—hence, the ambiguous presentation. This, thought Paul, at the cost of the dignity of all gay men.

"Do you think," he blurted out, "we would have been able to defend ourselves had they come over to us, those guys?"

The sound of his own voice surprised him. Because the subway car they had taken earlier that night had few available seats, several of the riders had to stand, including a trio of youths who stood together, near the door, speaking in elevated voices among themselves. Most of the passengers were either black or Latino, and ranged in age from the very young, five or six, for instance, to middle age. As it was late, however, no one seemed to notice anyone else. For that reason, Martin hadn't given it a moment's thought that maybe he should remain alert until the train reached their stop. It was only after he'd already done what he did that it struck him that he was taking a risk. But it was too late, then. So he decided to just "go with it." Someday, he thought, people would hardly pay attention to such things—just as most white people no longer raised an eyebrow, for instance, at seeing blacks seated at the front of the bus. The future had to begin somewhere. Why not with the two of them.

Disgusted with himself for his programmed attractions, Paul quickly lowered the magazine to his lap, to conceal his arousal.

"I don't know if we could have or not," Martin answered, flexing his wrists. "But I would have been happy to die trying."

He could feel Paul looking at him as if he had said something no one in their right mind would ever have said.

"You don't mean that. Tell me you don't mean that."

"I can't tell you what isn't so, can I? So, I won't."

"Jesus *fucking* Christ!"

Martin said: "Now you're angry at me. What did I say?"

Disgusted, the other man turned his back. He pulled up the bedclothes and once again pretended to fall asleep.

"It's simply my truth," Martin said after a while. As he spoke, he disturbed the air now and again with a flurry of fingers. "You should be happy I speak the way I do. Other people say other things, and for them it's their truth. But for me it isn't. It's simply my truth, Paul, that if anyone were to come up to me and tell me that I couldn't do what I do, be what I am, that I had to be, instead, like them, and do what they did—and if they were to strike me for it—then I would have to strike them back. And if one of us had to die in that exchange, then I would be happy to be that person, though I wouldn't prefer it. I'd *prefer* to be the one to live. Honestly, I would. Sometimes a person isn't able to choose his death, it just comes— like a phone call in the middle of the night. Or a concrete slab falling down on you from the sky—so suddenly you couldn't do anything, make any decisions or choices. If I could choose my death I'd choose to die for being myself—for being myself in the face of those who would say I couldn't, that I was an offense to their eyes. It's a thing to be proud of, Paul—not backing down from a choice like that. Not many people get the chance. Not that I'd want it, or I wouldn't be afraid; I would. But I wouldn't back down. I couldn't live with myself. I'd *want* to die, then."

While Martin was speaking, Paul rose slowly from bed. He went to stand before the rather ornate, expensive chest-of-drawers they'd invested in a few of years ago, after one of them had been promoted.

As he was listening, Paul picked up his silver-rimmed eyeglasses and secured them behind his ears. Pulling back the curtains from the window, he peered down at a couple, a man and a woman, strolling arm-in-arm on the street. The man, tall, with an easy-going, diffident manner, walked with his side pressed close to the woman's—apparently he was whispering some small lover's nothing into her ear—and she, in turn, stretched her smaller, lithe frame upwards to meet him, as if at some midway, neutral point. What he had to say to her was, of course, no one else's concern.

Nonetheless, for an instant, Paul tried reading the man's lips; however, it was too dark and he couldn't make out any words. For starters, he wanted to know if the things this couple said to one another were in any way different from the types of things he and Martin, during their own small intimate moments, said to one another. Simply, he wanted to learn if such differences might truly be a reason for others to cause bodily harm to him and the man he loved.

He followed the couple with his eyes until they had crossed Montague Street and had disappeared into one of the brownstones that lined the neighborhood. Their privacy, he thought, was sealed and completely uninvaded. That other people could inhabit the world so freely, and he and Martin could not angered him.

Paul turned from the window. "I don't like it that you say the things you do," he said, gesturing at Martin with his fist. "The things you say sometimes—Crazy, just crazy. I could kill you myself. With my bare hands. No one would know. I'd say you got sick and one day you simply didn't wake up. Everyone would believe me. Who'd doubt me in this day and age? No one, that's who. Oh, they'd feel sorry, for a while. Of course, they would. For a few days. A couple of weeks. They'd genuinely mourn. But, then, they'd let it go. They'd have to. My god. What else is there?"

In bed, Martin leaned far forward, to stretch his stiffening back. He was tired—not exactly like before, on the subway ride home earlier that evening after the play they'd seen, a new one by Suzan-Lori Parks, but tired nonetheless—and it was already 1 a.m. and he had to get up at 7, shower, dress, and be at City College by 9 o'clock. He wanted Paul to slip into bed next to him. It was cooler in their bedroom, not as cool as it would have been had the repairman come by to fix the broken air-conditioning unit, but cooler than an hour before; *that* was saying something. Now, at least maybe they would be able to rest.

"I'm not saying what I said to hurt you," Martin offered, in conciliation. "It's just very important for me to live in the world in a certain way. And to accept whatever consequences that come to me because of that choice. Not 'accept' exactly—That isn't the word; but you know what I mean. I want to be proud of myself. You can see that, can't you?"

"I see it," Paul said.

"You do?"

"Hell, yes. I just don't know if I could make the same choice, and stick by it. Or that I even necessarily believe in it. I don't know, Marty. It's as though if I don't believe in it I'm something less in your eyes."

"But you're not."

"Well, then, in my own. I don't think I like that."

Paul walked into the bathroom and looked at himself in the mirror, at the darkened circles around his eyes, and the freckles about his nose, which as a boy had made others call him "cute," or "white boy," but which as an adult only marked him as old—at only thirty-six—in the way that liver spots did for the elderly. Besides, he was also overweight and needed badly to diet. He thought of the question Martin had asked him, and which he had dodged: Why was he upset now, and not before? Perhaps it was only because he was getting older, and was noticing it. More and more, he felt the necessity to guard what little time he had left, not to expose it to any potential harm. To tread upon the earth lightly.

He splashed cold water on his face, and rinsed out his mouth. When he walked back into the bedroom, he realized Martin was waiting for him to finish what he had been saying.

Paul shrugged his shoulders.

"I don't know, Marty," he said, standing before the chest-of-drawers. "I feel as if I'm being judged somehow. That if I'm not willing to offer up my life, then I'm a coward. I *value* my life. My life's important to me. And I'd do anything to keep it. Maybe that makes me a coward. For one thing, for not wanting those guys on that train tonight to see us in a certain light, a light they might have difficulty seeing in, so to speak, and so would therefore feel the need to strike out at us—to darken things again, so that they could see themselves. It's all about self-interest, you know. That's all anything is: 'What *I* can get,' 'What's good for *me*,' and so forth. Forget the rest of us."

Martin nodded. "I know."

"Do you, really? I wouldn't want anything to happen to us. To what we have made together. It's something that's important to me, as my life is important. Is it so goddamn wrong to want to protect that, Marty, at whatever the cost—even at the cost of my dignity?"

Paul slid the drawer open and took out a small box of antacids. While he spoke, he punctured one of the foil packets and popped a tablet inside his mouth.

He said, chewing: "Don't take this the wrong way, Martin, but people like yourself—people who've always refused to let others define you, who are individualists—think it's easy to stand up to those who have something over you. Who can decide whether you live or die, or at the very least who can make you damn miserable because, for starters, how you think and how you live, as far as they're concerned, is such a godawful 'offense,' as you call it. I admire your indignation. Because it's my own. How could it not be? But what about those of us who aren't as brave, who haven't the courage you have to say 'Fuck 'em'? Who are afraid of losing the tiny bit of ground we've managed to gain in life? Why should we risk losing *that* for the sake of what other people are so righteously quick to call 'pride'? What's that word mean anyway? I confess, I never knew. Can a person be 'prideful' if he again and again offers the other cheek? Or ducks behind, say, a well-paying job, to avoid a life-threatening situation? I guess, what I'm asking—if I'm asking anything—is do we always have to *fight*? Can't we just refuse to? Just turn our backs and ignore the bastards—whomever 'they' are? Tell me, is that not an option anymore? And since when? I don't know, Marty, if you or anyone else has the right to condemn those content with what we have—not content with what we *want*, that's a different matter altogether: all of us *want* a heck of lot more than what any of us'll ever have—but content with what is *ours* already, what we've *earned*, by dint of our hard work, if just a bare minimum of ass-kissing?"

Getting out of bed, Martin stooped to pick up from the floor the fitness magazine Paul had earlier thrown at him. Martin tossed the magazine onto the chest-of-drawers and tried to place his arms around his agitated lover.

"Come to bed, baby," he said in a low voice. "It's late. Okay?"

But Paul jerked away. "Well, the hell with my dignity!" He slapped his palm heavily against his thigh. "Will my 'dignity' keep me warm at night? Will it listen to me when I've had a lousy day, having had to hold my tongue with those white liberals at work? Or stroke my ego when I look in the mirror and see yet another age line, or can pinch more than a half a foot off my waist? What if I *do* get sick. You know—with You-know-what? Where's my dignity going to help out when I can't hold my bowels, or forget to pull out my dick to take a piss, and so it streams in a warm bath down my fat, ugly ass thigh?"

"I don't have the answers, Paul. I don't know who does. Anyway, you're not fat or ugly. You could lose a few pounds. But that's all."

Martin turned off the nighttable lamp and slipped beneath the sheets. He waited for the other man, who continued to stand on the far side of the room, his arms folded stubbornly over his chest, to come to him.

"I'm too cool now," complained Paul, as he rubbed his arms.

Yawning, Martin patted the empty space on the mattress next to him.

"Come here," he said. "Like you said, it'll be morning soon, and we won't have slept. And then good heavens we'll look horrible. Something we *can't* have. We're fags, after all."

This last remark brought a slight smile to Paul's face, and his shoulders visibly loosened. Martin was relieved. After all, Paul wasn't like him, in that he had never grown up with other people pre-judging him because of the way he carried his school books, among other things. Or made disrespectful comments about girls one minute and then gone weak in the knees for one of them a minute later, like they did. Though he had often felt estranged from those around him on the inside, Paul had long ago learned to shape himself according to other people's specifications in order to belong. To fit in. And along the way he had earned rewards for doing so. But Martin, because of things that he had long believed were simply beyond his control (like, for instance, the way he used his hands when he spoke, fluttering in the air like bird's wings), had never been able to do that. Years ago he had tried several times to do so before he had finally just given up in frustration. It had been no use. He looked at the images of the nude men on the wall, looming over the two of them, and suddenly these old feelings of envy threatened to return. But it was late, he decided. Therefore, it was time to let go of troubling thoughts for which he had no resolution, and would likely never have any.

Martin shifted slightly when his lover slipped into bed next to him. He placed his head on Paul's shoulder after Paul had made himself comfortable. Next, he positioned one of his legs, bent at the knee, to nest in between Paul's legs, near the groin. One of Martin's arms lay pressed closely against his own side—the side onto which his slender frame was turned; the other, as usual, he flung across Paul's fleshy stomach.

Speaking in a hushed voice, Martin said: "I don't believe anyone can have what we have."

Paul sighed. "You don't?"

"No. They wouldn't deserve to have it as much."

"But then how is it that we deserve it?" Paul took his opposite arm and let it rest gently across Martin's ass.

"Because we took it and made it ours. No one gave us anything. It's like in that story, remember? Or was it a poem? That black gays are outlaws. 'Men in search of our own constitution.' That's us."

Paul flinched at the image.

"I know you don't like to think that way," said Martin.

Paul shook his head. "It's not that. It's just…. Well, it's just that I don't like to be romantic about my life."

"You think it's romantic?"

"I always did. But there's some truth to it, too. I don't have to like it."

The two men lay silent for a while, and listened to one another breathe. Finally, Paul reached over and switched off the lamp.

He said to his lover: "Put your head on my shoulder whenever you want. It's okay."

Martin's eyes had been closed. He opened them at hearing this, but he didn't smile.

"We'll talk about it in the morning," he said. "Good night."

Paul kissed him on the top of his head. "G'night, yourself."

Legacy

DAVID PUT DOWN HIS PENCIL AND WRINKLED HIS brow. It was not yet midnight. He slipped the sheet paper inside a nine-by-twelve manila envelope. On the face of the envelope, in large, neatly scripted letters, he wrote, "To my parents," and sealed it.

As he undressed, the final words Akutagawa had written in his suicide note came to him: "I have seen, loved, and understood more than others. In this, at least I have a measure of satisfaction, despite all the pain I have thus far had to endure."

Perhaps he should add the Japanese writer's apologia to his own letter, he thought, as a postscript; but that would be plagiarism. He simply repeated the passage to himself, hoping that such a sound, clearheaded resolve would strengthen his own. He had reason to doubt. Twice before, at the ages of twelve and twenty-nine, he had attempted to take his own life; each time, however, at the crucial moment, he had balked. Later, he had wondered why, when he was certain of his longing, he had failed. The only possible reason was that his soul, he concluded, was simply not prepared for its glory.

He walked through his tiny apartment, naked, wondering if things were different now. He stopped here and there to touch an object: a book, the woven fabric on his sofabed. Then he would move on. Like a giant slab of ancient stone, the parquet floor was cool and reassuring under his bare feet. He imagined his fossilized remains being dug out of that stone by a future archaeologist on the very spot where he was now contemplating his death. Perhaps his spirit, too, would be reincarnated into the body of that scientist, and coming upon its former life, as much as half a millennium later, the current one might suffer a tiny spasm of recognition; or a star, passing within the gravitational pull of a black hole, might simply explode, so that the escaped gases and the resulting radiation would unleash, in obvious homage, a well-timed burst of astral light.

"Imagine that," he thought.

David scratched at his pubic hairs; the rash there had spread to his navel—it was spiraling into him, like one of his father's silver-handled Black and Decker power tools. He could feel the disease wiggling its way through his lower duodenum to the valves of his heart. But it would never win; his was virtually an insurmountable lead. But he knew better than to slack off; after all, he had been practicing for this moment since he was a teenager. Nor would he let an exaggerated sense of his own invincibility outwit him as it had the rabbit in his disastrous race with the slow-moving tortoise. No, sir.

He thought—because he often thought of them—of his mother and father, and he decided that upon his death they should divorce one another and move to opposite poles of the vast earth. It was time that they each began fresh, stimulating lives. They should visit foreign countries and, it occurred to him, learn languages neither had known existed while they were married. And they should make love too, again and again, with always new and diverse partners: men and women as much unlike their former mates as possible. His old man, he decided, should read great books, only because he had not read any books before—Baldwin, Dostoevsky, Woolf—and he should familiarize himself with the age-old art of oratory. His mother, bless her heart, would do well to avoid reading altogether, and instead busy herself with paintings and sculptures, and works of imagination found helter-skelter in nature, such as the intricate patterns formed on the pellucid skin of fallen leaves in autumn. She would best strengthen her relationship to God and to herself in that way, and not through language. After all, even the simplest words had the tendency on occasion to cloud the moment of true knowing; whereas it was often, David had decided, just the opposite with silence.

And should his mother and father meet again, after a hundred or more years—either as man and woman, woman and woman, or man and man— they might try once more to come together in a loving union. Perhaps then, he thought, theirs might signal an omen of promise for the world. As it was, his parents' marriage seemed, to David, after thirty-odd years, to be a mere bringing-to-life of certain horrific scenes from Rodin's "Gates of Hell."

David sat at the edge of his bed. Burying his face in his hands, he tried to cry, but no tears would come. He heard a car drive by, then the shuffling feet of his next-door neighbors as they walked up the steps of their building. His name was Doug. His girlfriend, Padmaja, had moved from California to be with him. They were laughing and David tried to imagine his arms about their bodies, and theirs about his, all three of them shaking with laughter at the one joke. To picture this, he thought he would have to let go of everything else in his mind and will just this single, improbable image. He couldn't. He dropped his arms to the side of his body and, hearing their intimate movement through the thin walls, a bit of moisture then welled up in both his eyes. Who were they that they should do this to him, that he should do this to himself, that he should allow it even?

It was winter and after a while David began to shiver. He looked about the apartment. A draft must be seeping in through one of the windows. But he paled at the idea of delaying his suicide for the length of time it would take to close it. He glanced at the clock, where, next to his table lamp, a bottle of bright red pills sat with a tumbler of cool tap water.

It was ten minutes to midnight.

He turned the backs of his hands over and stared at the rapidly wrinkling skin of both his palms. Because of the cold, David could feel his scrotum sack, too, being drawn up tight inside his rectum. If he did not close the window then whoever found his corpse in the morning would go away with the mistaken idea that he had had, while alive, a tiny, shriveled, abnormally small penis. And worse, future biographers would refer to him always, as they had referred to the actor Montgomery Clift after his death, as "Princess Tiny Meat."

Always, the thought of his relatively small output of writing pained David. He sat there with this on his mind, shivering, unable to rise from the sofabed and close the window, so that, posthumously, his future celebrity would not be predicated on the rumor of a tiny dick. Poor, poor

Montgomery, he thought. What a legacy to leave behind! But at least there were the movies: *A Place in the Sun,* with violet-eyed Elizabeth Taylor. And *I Confess,* David's personal favorite. Those truly interested in the work could not be concerned with the dimensions of a man's sexual organ, he decided. However, he had yet to produce a substantial body of writing to deflect such perverse curiosity; therefore, in its absence, there would be only the hearsay of his infinitesimal member to gossip about.

He could not allow this. Rubbing his two palms together, David jumped up and searched quickly throughout his apartment for a sign of an opened window. He looked in the kitchen, in the bathroom, in the small room off his hall corridor where he wrote his derivative literary fragments; but every window was shut tight, no cold air from outside could possibly seep in. Therefore, he decided, the draft must have as its origin some divine, constantly shifting, incorporeal location. Possibly it was the same draft that had saved him from swallowing enough aspirin to do irreparable harm to himself when he was a boy; the same draft too that had convinced him, when he was twenty-nine, not to plunge headlong off the George Washington Bridge simply because a story of his had been rejected for an anthology of writings by black gay men.

Maybe, he mused, it was not his time to die. After all, he had not seen the continent from whence his mysterious ancestors had come, emaciated and slick with their own excrement, nor had he stared long enough at any still life painting by Cézanne.

And who had he loved besides that one man?

Who?

And hadn't he been the one to ruin that? What was his name now?

David began to shiver at first imperceptibly, and then with more violence. He reached down to scratch his groin. Without thinking, he fingered the rash that was, he assumed, slowly disemboweling him, twisting into his body like Mishima's *seppuku* sword. He pushed his penis aside and stared at the dozens of miniscule blisters in between the coarse hairs. The burning and itching reminded him of the inflammation he had suffered in high school his junior season on the wrestling team. According to his coach, the irritation was nothing more serious than an ordinary case of jock itch. Following the older man's advice, David picked up an over-the-counter remedy from the pharmacy in the suburban neighborhood where he lived then with his parents. After a week the soreness and the bumps cleared up, as did the itching.

David thought aloud to himself: "It can't be the same thing. Can it?"

He looked at the clock. The drug stores were closed at this hour. And most likely Doug and Padmaja had already fallen asleep; besides, they didn't seem the athletic types. Absentmindedly, David touched the palm of his right hand to his chest, to his stomach, to his throat, to both his cheeks. He was ravenous. He had not swallowed a morsel of food the entire day, perhaps fearing he might defecate on himself at the moment of death. This, he decided, was the same humiliation his dignified forefathers and mothers must have suffered, as many of them, their faces animated too by panic, plunged off slave ships by the hundreds into a shark-infested Atlantic Ocean. His own logic at the time was that if he did not eat, then there would be no waste in his body at the final moment to excrete. He laughed at the absurdity of his reasoning, and thought: "You're one funny bastard, Kunta Kinte! 'No chicken, no chicken shit.' You crack me up."

Picking up his briefs from beside the sofabed, David stepped into them and went into the kitchen. Inside the refrigerator he found half an enchilada and slipped it inside the microwave to warm up. Tomorrow he would visit the pharmacy near where he worked, in Rockefeller Center, and see about an ointment for his rash. If that failed—he touched the palm of his left hand to his check, his right palm to his stomach, and both, simultaneously, as in a prayer, to his throat—then he would take the HIV test.

Maybe.

The Confessions of John-Paul Simmons

Transcribed by the author

(The following is a letter that was given to me by a relative, someone who worked as a nurse at the mental hospital in Albany, New York, where John-Paul Simmons was treated off and on for several years. The letter has no intended addressee. It was addressed as is, handwritten and folded into a yellowing envelope and undated. I have transcribed the letter just as it was written. All I have done is to add paragraphing and standardize the spelling. Otherwise, the letter is just as I found it. John-Paul Simmons was the husband of Dawn Langley-Simmons, a white British writer who had been born male but had a sex-change surgery sometime in the late 1960s. John-Paul Simmons died in 2003. His former wife died in 2000.)

To Whom It May Concern:

I can remember the day I began to lose my mind. It was the day when the white man I had been sleeping with told me that he planned to change his sex and become a woman, all so that the two of us could marry and be husband and wife. Up until that time I am convinced that I had been the sanest of men. My mother tells me this even today, when she comes to visit me here in the hospital, something she does the third Sunday of every other month. She brings me the *Archie* comics I like to read, and a box of Reese's peanut butter cups. I have always had what we call a sweet tooth. My teeth are no longer good. In fact, I haven't got many of them left. This is why I seldom smile these days. I used to be quite a good-looking young man. But now I look like a man twenty, thirty years older than I am. It is all because of that woman. Of course I mean because of that man. All these years and I am still doing her bidding. She really had me trained, I will give her that. I loved her when she was a man. But I had come to hate him when he became a woman. How to explain that? How can a person love someone because of the sex they happen to be and come to hate that person when the sex they are no longer matches the sex they were? It is a mystery to me.

You see, I am a Negro. And I will always be a Negro. There is no changing that fact, at least no way that *I* know of. And in the part of the South where I was born Negroes do not mingle with whites in the way that men mingle with women. And we certainly do not mingle with white men who transform themselves into white women. For that is a blasphemy before God. I was told this by somebody I knew back in Charleston; I forget who. Though later, when I went combing through the Bible in my mother's house for evidence I was unable to find any. I remember wondering if this meant that person had lied to me. In those days I did not have a close relationship to God. I was a heathen. A non-believer. I still do not know if I believe in Him. If He exists, He gave me something no man should have a right to, and then He took it away. What kind of God would do such a thing to a poor Negro like me? I haven't done anything to nobody. Never did.

I tried to stay away from Gordon—that was his name, you know… before. But he kept finding me and telling me how much he loved me. How much he needed me. He would do anything to make me happy, he said. No white person, no white *man*, certainly, had ever dared say such words to me before. I thought, My God. This here is a white man telling me these things. Surely the resurrection has come! I felt special to be the one to hear those words. Like Mary Magdalene. I was a Negro, after all. She was a whore. We Negroes did not hear such things from whites. I think that is why I came to love him in the end. Because he chose to give himself to me in this way. He chose to make himself naked and strip off his white skin so that it no longer held the power it once had. Gordon gave up his white skin for me. But he did not ask me to give up my black skin. And so I kept it. So there we were: a Negro and a white man who was no longer white but skinless, no longer a man but a woman. I think that was why he had decided to change his sex. It would have been too difficult for him to live that way. Without skin. But if he turned himself into a white woman, then it would not be the same as being a white man. This would have been an impossible love. A white man and a black man? Who would have believed such a thing in those days? No one, that's who.

If Gordon became a woman the two of us would be equal in a way. But not exactly equal, if you know what I mean? I mean, I would be the man, then, and he, Gordon, would be the woman. It would be alright then, he told me. Wouldn't it, Johnny? No one would care then, would they? And we could be happy, the two of us. Man and woman, husband and wife, and not simply black man and white man. Not only an abomination, but against custom. I have to admit, I liked that part. I liked it a lot. We could go and live someplace where to be a mixed couple was not such a problem. There were places you could do that in those days. A few places anyway. So I thought, Yes, we could do that. But then I slept on it and when I awoke and told Gordon no, that it would not do, he said, calmly, fine, you're right, Johnny. I don't know what I was thinking. Forget it. And that was that. Or so I thought. But when he went away for a couple of weeks (it might have been longer)—to do research on a book he was writing, he said—and came back dressed in women's clothes, I thought my world had crashed. I thought, Nigger, what mess have you got yourself into with this faggot cracker?

He told me he'd had the operation. When he lifted his dress back at our place, I saw that his ding-a-ling was gone. In its place I saw a square adhesive bandage, all bloody, that covered over what he would come to call his 'woman's business.' I cried for weeks. I would not let him—her— touch me. I wanted no part of such madness. God made the body, not man. It did not matter that I didn't believe in God. I knew the words; they were inside me. So I used them.

Gordon had made himself into a God. The type of God I had never known could exist. A Man-Woman-God. After a while I realized that if this were so, if Gordon was now a God, and if Gordon loved me like he said he did, then what that meant was that I was loved by a God—a man who had become a God by miraculously becoming a woman. What Negro whose people had been enslaved by white devils turned down a God's love? A foolish Negro, that's who. And my mother didn't raise no fools.

No sir. Not here. Not anywhere. So I just got up off my high-horse and let myself be loved by the white man who was no longer a white man but who was instead a God in the body of a masculine-looking white woman with hairy armpits. Oh yes. And for a time I considered myself one of the blessed few.

We got married, just like Dawn—that was Gordon's name now—wanted us to. And we were happy. Newspapers came to interview us. We were on television a couple of times. Dawn wrote a couple of new books. We lived grand lives for a time. But then she started talking about having a baby. I'm ready to be a mother, Johnny, she told me. My biological clock's ticking, is what I remember her saying. I mean, I know I said she was a God and all, but a white woman with hairy armpits, especially a white woman who used to be a white man, does not give birth to babies. I know I was not the smartest of men, but I knew that much. But then Dawn began to put on weight. Her belly actually swelled. I saw it when she would get undressed at night. I saw it with my own Negro eyes. When the baby was born—Dawn went away to have it; she would not let me come with her—everything changed for us. She became a stranger to me. I thought to myself, Who are you? Who am I? Who is this child you have named Natasha after a character in a Russian novel? Where is the God you were and who is this devil in my bed at night? After this, the mind I had once believed I was losing suddenly began to feel lost again. I could not find it, though I tried. You have to believe me. I did try. It has now been many years since that time. Dawn, I hear, has died. Natasha is a mother herself now. And I am writing this letter to you from deep inside my insanity.

Yours truly,
John-Paul Simmons

Immortally Yours

A CLOSE FRIEND IS GETTING MARRIED IN TWO days. Mondale (no relation whatsoever to Fritz) is heterosexual, but that detail has never mattered to either of us; or, rather, to him. On my end, relocating to another state is what has made it matter less. This was the sole purpose of moving. It is quite okay that he does not acknowledge it in the way I do—acquiescence comes with the territory; it is a fact I have come to accept, and not wrestle with.

This is how I am. My Manhattan friends call me "The Cushion" because of the way I absorb the brunt of romantic entanglements with white men. They are amazed at how complimentary I can be toward these "Caucasoids" who, in their eyes, do nothing but use me up. Calmly, I ask them where is the advantage in resenting these fellows? Whatever is heaped upon me is because somewhere along the line I've obviously invited it. Those past lovers were only performing roles scribbled in my own karmic ink many centuries ago. But a non-comedic belief in past lives is not a trait shared among us, so the topic seldom comes up.

And anyway, Mondale was never one of those spiritual boy-toys. He drew the line at that point and, in order to remain his friend I knew not to cross it, not to push his homosexual panic button. Yet, if I regret anything in my current life it is this position of being a tangent in his world, forever stepping on his heels.

I am, by Mr. Webster's book definition and by my own say-so, a coward for letting things continue in this way. It was never necessary that I reply to his letters, to play advisor when society and women gave him the runaround blues. I should have struck a match to each of them without opening a single envelope. But I never learned to resist his handwriting and therefore read and promptly answered every one— including the invitation to this most inconsiderate of weddings. What can I say except that I am bound to perpetuate things as they are? Mondale and I will forever be confined to the reasons separating us. He will marry on Sunday this female he refers to in his bi-monthly letters as Sharon or Shari, or whatever it is he calls her, and I will continue searching for his replacement, someone who has his look of bewilderment on the face, a little boy's expression of being always lost.

He tells me his name is Tim—not Timmy or even Timothy, but Tim— and he has, next to Mondale, this century's most uninformed smile. We spoke while in line for 6:30 p.m. train tickets to Washington, though he is traveling only as far as Wilmington, Delaware. A girl behind us joined the conversation when he half-jokingly referred to himself as a pessimist, seeing as the clock read 6:20 and we still had not purchased tickets. She confirmed his guess that we could buy them on the train, if push came to shove, for only a few dollars extra. Intuitively, I knew Tim was her perfect match and so gave them my back for a while; but when he touched my sleeve and made a joke, a not particularly funny joke, I knew it was all right to face them again. My laughter on the flat punch line put her off—I could tell this as she took a quarter-step backwards and somewhat distractedly re-counted her two twenty dollar bills.

It is 6:29 by the clock over the escalator, one minute until the conductor pushes the button for the train to leave the station. I am holding one of the doors open in case he makes it. I need to be certain we'll sit together; and since he is not really my friend yet, I could not with any degree of comfort wait while he paid for his ticket with that woman behind him listening in. To relax, I tap my feet in a staccato to the internal rhythms I always hear in my ears. A second later, I breathe air into my palm and cup it to my nose for possible signs of halitosis. A young girl in an Afro-cut drags her child behind her while looking into my eyes. Where is the baby's daddy, I ask her with my eyes. Why isn't his face clean? But she ignores my intrusion with a glance of her own that says, Hi! Wanna be my husband and pay my bills?

I turn away from her when I see Tim coming down the escalator with his duffel bag in tow. And when I see that he is alone and not with his "most perfect match," I lean against the door and let the sweat bumps break out freely over my back. It is happening again, and I will do everything in my power to aid it. As he walks toward me, I take notice of how similar the hairstyle is to Mondale's: it is neither Ivy League nor metropolitan, but college-boy suburban. The fact that he has no lips is minor, since he has plenty of teeth to make up for this deficiency.

He is behind me as we dodge fellow passengers in the aisle. I am looking for a needle in a haystack trying to find two seats together; but, since he is the pessimist, I know there is hope for our future when, on his own, he spots an empty pair further to the left of us. He arranges his duffel bag and smaller knapsack on the overhead rack. When he is finished, I ask him to find room for my things and he does. These early moments between us seem promising if the pace remains unrushed and casual. I take the window seat and as soon as he's down he jumps up and asks if I want anything from the bar. Without hesitating, I answer "No thanks," but he brings me back a Molson Golden anyway—this first one being on him, he says.

It is perhaps too easy to pick out the resemblances between the two, especially since each passing thorn bush outside my window is bringing me closer to Mondale. In addition to the hair and nearly pink-rose complexion, they grip beer bottles in the same way: with the neck wedged firmly in the vertex of the thumb and forefinger and the other three digits drumming against the bottle. The edges of Tim's nails are ragged from chewing. Mondale, because he is a worrier, also bites his off instead of using clippers. He once told me, years ago when we worked on our college newspaper together, that brittle nerves made him chew at them. I can see him now, pacing in his apartment on Longfellow Street in Washington, second-guessing his every decision about marrying this woman.

Tim tells me he is an actor, and instantly the connection is made. Many of my Manhattan friends are in the wonderful world of show business: dancers, actors, singers—some are even unlucky enough to be all three. However, these friends, unlike Tim and Mondale who ravage their nails, suppress their disappointment and worry behind overlarge smiles, scented musk oils, and the Buddhistic healing powers that come from chanting for hours at a stretch "namyohorengekyo." I often, when in a room with these individuals, find it soothing trying to decipher the crossword puzzle of their colorful gestures and words.

In time, Tim speaks to me of partying, and then specifically of his long-standing involvement with the other sex. He is twenty-two, he says, and hardly a weekend goes by that he does not get disgustingly drunk and lay one of them. Having nothing to add to these anecdotes, I only nod my head. I cannot pretend, and this has always been a major blemish according to my Manhattan friends. But they can simply go to hell. I will not compromise myself and fake enthusiasm just so a man will like me. If a nod of the head won't do, then so be it. Besides, I am much too sober right now to act any other way. I grip the neck of my Molson's and take an extra long swig—maybe it will help to relax me. But Tim changes the direction of the conversation anyway, and speaks to me of how close the trains pass one another along the track, of how fast the speeds must be.

We finish our beers and he is up again. This time I give him a few dollars, it being my round to buy, and turn to watch him go down the aisle behind me. This man is handsome in his own right, but my reasons for wanting him have little to do with the soul eddying beneath the brown hair and pale skin. He will remain infinitely unknowable to me, just as the other white faces who've reminded me of Mondale all have. Yet my city friends are quick to blame these ex-lovers. After all, we see too much of one another to unleash harsh character judgments, no matter how to the point. It would be too risky when we depend so pathetically on the camaraderie of our little informal group.

But, regardless of them, I know myself far too well to be surprised by any of my own choices. In fact, I might suggest, as a way of teasing Tim, that we exchange phone numbers when he returns. All things considered, my eyes are wide open in this thing, and they will stay that way until the second coming of our Lord and Savior Jesus Christ, when perhaps we will all be rescued from the merry-go-round of our lives.

After a while I sense Tim and cock my head to the right. He is smiling that neon smile and extending a second Molson towards me. I watch him hitch the fabric of his tan trousers at the thigh and sit. For the first time in over an hour, I smell him. The scent is of grass and wind. Upon sitting, he tells me that, in addition to acting, he models and also does landscaping to round out his income. I take a drink from my bottle, laugh, and slap, quite by reflex, the top of his knee. This second beer is much too confident and gushes through my system like nobody's business. We talk more about the world in general and I tell him of the afternoon I gave a homeless man a five dollar bill, only to have him chase me a whole city block protesting about it being too large a sum.

Before long, Tim is back on the subject of vaginas and tells me of the time he screwed one on his front porch while his father mowed the lawn not fifteen feet in front of them. She sat sideways on his lap, he says. It was a Sunday in July and both their families were at home, so there was no alternate place to go. They positioned themselves on a swinging bench and he stroked her hair while she pretended to be asleep. He came so hard, he tells me, that he swears some cum bubbled out of the ear she had on his shoulder. I pull my jacket over my lap to conceal my sudden erection. Tim doesn't have a jacket and his knapsack is overhead, so he uses his forearms as a modest shield.

Because of the mature themes of our conversation, he can no longer respond to me as an innocent, as he could at the beginning of this scenic train ride. I tell him I have to take a leak and he gets up to let me cross. Out of habit, he stretches his legs in the aisle, momentarily forgetting his own protruding condition, and smiles sheepishly; while I, feeling expectedly triumphant, foam at the mouth and head for the bathroom.

Once inside, I lean against the wall of the tiny compartment while my urine streams down into the silver platter. Some of the urine washes up and around the base and swirls to the floor. Without inhibition I take my semi-erect dick and point it at the back wall and spray-pee Tim's name on the blue paint. I have enough fluid left to spell "Tim" out three times. When finished, I look into the mirror over the tin sink and see how droopy my expression has become. The beer has depleted the muscle tone in my face and torso, and now everything above my waist has dropped below my belt. I want to masturbate, but Tim will be getting off soon and I cannot waste any of our time together. I wash my hands, dry them, and pull back the metal latch.

Tim is waiting for me as I walk the short distance down the corridor. He has the aisle seat and can study me from head to tennis shoes. Like me, he has noted the time and is not smiling now, but considering the possibilities. And before I can even sit, the speakers come on and a bearish voice announces Wilmington as the next stop. This time Tim does not stand but stays put, with his eyes fixed on the food tray in front of him, and motions for me to scoot my black ass low across his lap to reach my own seat.

"You know, we oughta get together, dude," he says, "seeing how you like movies as much as me." (We never discussed anything of the sort.) "Man, I'll see anything, you know: foreign films, comedies, dramas, romance—you name it. You got any paper?"

I open up my shoulder bag and take from there the pad and pen I keep for these predestined meetings and hand them over. Though Tim is right-handed, I notice he slants the pen awkwardly, the same as Mondale, who writes with his left. I can easily see him growing up in Wilmington, with the train tracks so near to his parents' house. I could even paint a watercolor, if called upon, of him and his buddies trekking across blacktop avenues, and the girls eyeing them and becoming slaves because of these boys' looks.

I take the pad and pen from his hands and scribble down my own vital statistics. I then tear the sheet off and fold it so he cannot read it right away, and put it into his shirt pocket myself. No one can see us clearly and so he lays his palm over mine and mentally strokes my skin. Again, he does not smile, and out of mock consideration neither do I. I want, in fact, to laugh out loud when his left eye goes moist, and not because I am unsentimental or lack that type of feeling myself. But because I know far too much about *everything* these days to become weak in the joints at the sight of a good-looking man near tears.

I probably won't even cry at Mondale's wedding. So what if his marriage sends me reeling further out among the stars than even I expected? One day he'll come to his senses and realize he all the time belonged with me, and not Cheryl or whatever the mugambo her name is. And when he does, all he'll need do is whisper my name and, like a comet streaking through infinity, I'll *zing* right back into his arms. But…

…now, in order to catalogue this one's face and identity with at least some uniqueness, I have refrained from writing either my correct address or legitimate last name on that torn slip of notepad; and what I did write was not legible. I will, through Tim, have my own fun and stretch out a long-wished-for fantasy of being sought after but never found. I want desperately to pick up the *Village Voice* and see, week after week, year after year, the following message printed on the back page:

> (5/23 Amtrak to Wash.) You: Jamal, a Native Son in blk
> jeans. Me: Tim, a Tom Cruise type. You liked my longer
> hair & we drank 2 Molsons. Exchanged #s but can't
> read your writing. Pls call actor enroute to Delaware.
> 874-6342.

Tim gets up before the train stops completely and unloads his duffel bag and knapsack from overhead. For the public at large we shake hands and say we'll get in touch for that movie or something. I can tell he doesn't want this to be the end by his furtive glances toward my seat while he waits for the brakes to catch; but, like Mondale, he is uninformed and does not realize that this isn't, not by a long shot, one of those predictable, see-ya-soon kind of goodbyes. Oh, no. In fact, it ain't a goodbye at all. Because when the seeds I've planted in Tim ripen, he'll find himself, quite unexpectedly, on the lookout for…well, if not me, then someone reincarnated to look like me, a snow queen dressed in my clothes maybe, with my look of false calm about the face and all that rigmarole.

Ordinary Life

WHEN I WAS SIXTEEN MY FATHER DIED SUDDENLY, and three months later, at the beginning of spring, my mother began to seriously entertain the notion of marrying her hairdresser. Phil Wilson was an obese man, with a bald spot and L-shaped sideburns. He stood a whole foot shorter than my old man, who at 6'5" tall had nearly become the first Negro to be drafted into professional basketball, in 1950; that distinction would go instead to Chuck Cooper, out of Duquesne University, while my Dad went off to fight in the Korean War. A lifetime devotee of the sport, my father would often goad me into a game of one-on-one with him—though this was hardly the game I most enjoyed—and dribbling the ball in between both his legs and mine, he'd shoot over my flailing arms to score a basket. I can still hear his menacing, deep-voiced laughter in my head, taunting me as I sleep: "You got shit on your dick or what, boy? *Mooove!*" Sparks of saliva would, then, fly from his mouth into my face, and I'd knuckle down and toss the ball to him for the next shot.

Phil Wilson, on the other hand, never asked me to play sports with him, nor slapped me on the back so hard that my shoulder would ache for days. He could not walk up a flight of stairs without stopping in the middle for a gasp of breath. In our small community, men like Phil Wilson were often scorned and ridiculed for what other people thought of as their "unnatural" ways. In Phil's case, he was a man who straightened and curled his own hair, when he'd had hair, just as he did his lady customers, and who sometimes doused himself too liberally with sweet-smelling cologne. But these were not things that mattered to me. Simply, after my father died and Phil Wilson started coming to our house, I felt a weight inside me lift. And as if by magic my school grades improved. I even got up the courage to ask out the girl I liked most at the time, Sandra Brown. It was a happy time.

One afternoon I came upon Phil Wilson slumped on the sofa in our house on Tenth Street, in Richmond, Virginia, which is where my mother and I lived then. This was not something unusual; Phil would often drop by midday, with the most recent fashion magazines, such as *American Girl, Glamour, Vogue*. He and my mother would then turn the pages together, each commenting about which style would look best on her, and which wouldn't. At my approach, Phil looked up and all of a sudden burst into tears. I dropped my school books onto the coffee table and sat next to him. I tried to wrap my arms around his humongous shoulders, in a show of comfort, but it was like trying to embrace a mountain.

"It's going to be A-okay," I said, patting him on the back. "You just let it out, Phil. Go on. You let it out now, ol' buddy."

Phil Wilson was dressed in his sky-blue beautician's smock. The fabric had worn through years of use so that you could see the rolls of flesh bunched up underneath, like the hard, swollen lumps of overdone grits. His hands smelled of Bergamot scalp treatment and singed hair from the long, stuffy afternoon spent in his shop. However, his nails were immaculate, as always, which he kept neatly trimmed and painted a fair shade of orchid pink.

My mother, I noticed, was nowhere in sight.

I had not been a witness to human grief before my father's death. As my parents' only child, I was brought up to be an adult, and as such they had instilled in me from an early age the necessity to avoid strong feeling—of course, unless in the heat of competition, my father would say. Because of these values, I seldom had opportunity to experience, first-hand, the more passionate emotions. That is, until my father's funeral.

On that day, several women I did not know had erupted into a series of mournful cries of affection for my father. Almost in unison, they shouted out his name, their words choked back with mucous: "*Jim*! Jim, baby, I *love* you!" Throughout, as was our nature, my mother and I remained in our seats, with our hands clasped dignified and stoic in our laps. Even when the final shovel of topsoil had been thrown atop the coffin, our expressions remained unchanged. Several times, however, I managed to steal glances at these anonymous women, who were eventually comforted by my father's cronies, men whose wives were not present for one reason or another, or who were divorced already; or men who had never been married and so who would presumably always be "bachelors of the heart," as my father had at one time referred to them. These were men my Dad had played pickup games with at my high school gymnasium on weekends, and with whom he sometimes drank beer for hours at a stretch in our living room, so that I could not concentrate on my schoolwork, a thing that was important to me in those days.

That afternoon I took Phil Wilson's hand in my own, as I had seen my father's cronies do with those women, and I stroked and kneaded his bloated flesh.

"It's gonna be all right, Phil," I repeated, lowering my voice, though I didn't yet know what the matter was.

He gripped my hand tight in his and began to rock his large body forward and back.

"It's a dark day for this child of Adam, Juney," he said.

"What d'ya mean, Phil?" I asked. "Where's my Momma?"

Strands of shorn hair lay scattered across the face of his smock. And peroxide stains, combined with the toxic fluid from dyes and lye-based relaxers, further discolored the cloth. Phil Wilson took up the ends of the fabric in his hands and blew his nose.

"She says No-can-do, boy," he said, waving his thick wrist in the air, as if swatting at flies. "Your Momma come 'round the shop 'bout three p.m. and give me back my ring. I'm loading stock just received from New York City, when Marguerite hollers out back wit her loud mouth-self: 'Phil! Yo' No. 1 customer's out front!' Right away I know who that is. Shoot, who else could be ol' fat Phil's No. 1 customer but yo' Momma, right?"

Phil Wilson stood up then, and walked across the room. Over the fireplace sat a daguerreotype of my father's father, and next to him my mother had placed a military portrait of my Daddy, when he was in the Air Force, taken several years before I'd been born. Phil flexed his stubby arms, and snorted. All at once the color drained from his cheeks, and the hard rolls of skin at the base of his neck expanded accordion-like as he breathed. With his leathery lips turned down at the corners, he hunched his shoulders and stared into my father's portrait. He started to growl—a low, rumbling, in-the-throat sound I'd heard from neighborhood dogs. This continued without pause for a full minute. When he faced me, bright bubbles of sweat were rolling down his forehead and temples, and disappearing into his bushy sideburns. For a moment I was frightened—not for myself, but for him. Finally, Phil Wilson raised his fists to the ceiling, clasped his hands together, and quoted in an agonized voice from what I recognized as the 22nd Psalm:

> My God, my God, why hast thou forsaken me? Why art thou so far from helping me, and from the words of my roaring?

All of this was a novelty to me. I had not been born into a religious household. Except for attending church services on Easter Sunday, and for my father's funeral, I had not worshipped God with any regularity. As far as I could see, He owed me nothing; nor did I feel the need to request anything. We lived in completely separate worlds, God and myself; I didn't see the use for Him, though it was clear that other people certainly did—for instance, Phil Wilson. Up to that point, little in my life had prepared me for the sight of a grown man snarling, as if he were a German Watchdog warning of an intruder, at a photograph of a dead person, and then joining his hands together afterwards to plead for divine mercy. I did not know what was expected of me, if anything. I simply sat on the sofa with my hands clamped firmly between my knees, and thought to myself: All this will pass, and I will go upstairs to my bedroom, as I'd planned to do, and change into my street clothes, and meet my girl.

After a while, Phil Wilson unlaced his hands and wiggled his fat body out of his blue, beautician's smock. He balled the garment into a bundle and dragged it across his heavily perspiring neck and forehead. Then, looking over at me, a little shy, he grinned, and I saw his silver tooth glitter from the inside of his deep mouth, like a kind of hidden treasure.

"You think 'ol Phil's crazy as a cockroach, doncha, boy? I bet that's what you be thinking over there, with your pressed corduroys on, and your cherry-red lips. Say it. Say: '*Girl*, you crazy! Come on. Don't be a fraidy cat."

"No, Phil," I said. "That wouldn't be a nice thing to say. You got a lot on your mind, is all."

He looked at me, still grinning, though the expression in his eyes was vacant, and moved across the room. As though suspicious about something, he slipped a finger into the blinds and peeked onto the street. He wheeled around sharply and tossed the soiled smock into a chair.

"It's a cruel world we livin' in, boy," he said. "Don't let nobody tell you different. Why, to hear her tell it, your Momma never loved me: 'I never loved you, Phillip-Lee,' she said. Just as cold-hearted as a snake. Then she placed the ring in my hand, smoothed her palms over her long, luxuriant hair—the same luxuriant hair I been stylin' to the very best of my powers for the past fifteen years—and left. She just left ol' fat Phil."

"But she *likes* you, Phil," I said. "She doesn't like anybody as much."

Phil Wilson reached back and touched the slick patch of his bald spot.

"Ah, well," he said, calmly. "This is yo' Daddy's work, this is. He don't want yo' Momma to be happy. So like that magician-fella, Howdini, he's found a way to come back from beyond the grave. Delores won't admit it, of course, but I'd bet my silver tooth it's the gospel truth. I bet yo' Daddy's been lying in bed wit us every night. That's why I, that's why—"

He faltered here, and shifted his large body to stare up again at the portrait of my father above the fireplace. He even jabbed his finger towards it.

"I don't mean no disrespect, Juney. Lord knows, I'm a God-fearing man. But I wouldn't put it past yo' Daddy to have made a pact wit Lucifer, hisself, to get what he wants. For instance, I don't doubt for a *minute* he ain't in this room *right* now—right this *very* minute—stirring up trouble in yo' innocent breast against ol' fat Phil Wilson."

Here, with an amazing lightness, Phil Wilson pirouetted about the room on the balls of his wide feet. He raised his voice when he spoke.

"*Is that true, Jim? You in this house? You here?*"

He blinked his eyes, and waited. For several moments, Phil Wilson peered out into the dim room, as if fully expecting some otherwordly reply. Getting none, he then scratched under his chin and looked at me.

"You feeling any different 'bout ol' pig-face? I wouldn't blame you, boy, if you did. After all, you is his one and only. His rightful heir, and splittin' image. Flesh of his flesh, as the Good Book says. His blood runs through your body like hell-fire. There's no escaping that fact."

Listening to him, I drew my legs up to my chin and wrapped my arms about my legs, like I did when I was younger and my mother and father were fighting.

"I look like my Momma, Phil," I said. "Forgive me, but everybody says so. Even Sandra, my girl. Shoot, she says I've got my mother's eyes and nose. Even her way of tilting her chin up to heaven when she's upset about something and can't for nothing talk about it."

I stared up at the photograph of my father.

"Dead is dead, Phil," I said. "Houdini ain't coming back, nor is my Daddy. I don't want to look like him. Don't say I do when I don't, okay?"

At this, Phil Wilson pursed his lips and arched his dark eyebrows. An awful look came over him and I feared he might topple over and I'd have to lift his heavy body, stiffening with rigor mortis, from the floor. The whites of his eyes glazed over and his neck swelled to what seemed to me an unnatural size. I remembered that on the day of my father's funeral his own eyes had been artificially sewn shut; it was something that was done to the dead, I had been told: to prepare them for their next life, which didn't require looking at things and judging them in the same, distant way that people who were alive had to. On that day, leaning over my father's body, I thought: This is death, and in time it comes to each of us. Not a bad thing, just something that must be reached, and then hopefully surpassed; or not. That part wasn't exactly a guarantee. Staring down at my father I saw a thin cord of white stitching along the lower portion of his eyelids. This surprised me, because I had not expected death to be hand-tailored, in the way that a suit was hand-tailored: patterned to fit certain measurements, and not others. And although it happened to everyone, death, it was also a completely individual matter—people died differently, just as they lived differently. This suggested to me that there could be forces in some lives that were stronger than in others, and which might pass on after the natural decaying of their own bodies into other people—for instance, their children. In life, my father had been a powerful man. And for a host of reasons—the least being his lost youth— he had also been a bitter one. I assumed that death had made him less powerful, and his bitterness not such a threat to my happiness, or to my mother's. But maybe I was naïve. Simply stitching together the eyelids of a person who had died did not necessarily promise to put an end to a man's lifelong disappointment. And unless precautions were taken, that person's unresolved conflicts could break the nylon threads and transfer themselves to the nearest living surrogate. In other words, just as Phil had suspected, the dead, through the living, *could* rise again and rage forth.

Just then I left Phil Wilson standing in the middle of the floor and raced up the stairs to my mother's bedroom. It had not occurred to me that she was even inside the house. I simply had to get away, and clear my head. However, when I opened the door, my mother lay upon her floral-print bedspread, with her palms folded evenly atop one another. Her long, auburn hair was parted down the center and fanned out against the cotton pillowcase, like Julie Christie's hair, an actress in the movie I'd seen with Sandra on our first date. At that time, my mother favored a type of eyeliner called "Frosty Whites," she'd seen advertised in *Ebony* magazine, which when applied above the lashes reminded me of the nylon threading stitched along my father's eyes. She lay utterly still. And except for a streak of late afternoon sunlight outside my mother's window, the room was in complete darkness.

"What you thinkin', Junior?" she asked, the sound of her voice actually startling me. "You figure Phillip-Lee down there know what he's huffin' on 'bout when he says your Daddy done come back? You believe in that supernatural hogwash, d'you?"

I moved further into the room and sat down at the foot of my mother's bed.

"I don't know, Momma."

"You don't know?" Her voice had a soft lilt, when she spoke, so that I often thought of the line about "turtle doves," in the Christmas song. "*Chile!* You don't know what you believe? You just *like* your Momma, ain't you? I swear, don't know what *I* believe neither. Never did. But I know one thing, boy."

She tilted her chin.

"What's that, Momma?"

"I know I can't marry that man, Junior. Ghost or no ghost. I can't. I just can't. And don't ask me for reasons, 'cause Lord *knows* I ain't got one."

"I understand, Momma."

"You do?"

"I think so."

"Glad somebody does."

We fell into silence, and just listened to one another breathe up all the air in the room we could: just *suck* it up. Sitting in a corner, I saw a collection of my father's sports trophies he'd won as a boy, and a jersey he always claimed he'd gotten from the great William "Pop" Gates when he'd come through Richmond with the Tri-Cities Blackhawks, in the late 1940s. A pair of scruffed up All-Star Converse sneakers—size thirteen— also sat propped against the curved leg of my Momma's vanity table. On the table itself, lay a pile of faded photographs of my parents at the time of their marriage—photographs which had not been put away since my father's memorial service, nearly three months earlier.

After a while, my mother and I could hear Phil Wilson jumping up and down atop the furniture in our living room, smashing lamps to the floor, and snorting like a wild rhinoceros. He started up again with his Psalm:

All they that be fat upon the earth shall eat and worship:
all they that go down to the dust shall bow before him:
and none can keep alive his own soul!

I climbed, then, into bed with my mother and stretched my body alongside hers, on the side my father had slept on, before he passed away; the side, too, on which Phil Wilson had made himself comfortable when he had stayed over nights and I suspect found that he was unable to make love to a woman, though he wanted nothing else as badly. Whether this failure was primarily due to my father menacing him, from beyond the grave, as it were, or for a completely different reason, one I knew nothing of, was of little importance to me.

In time, my mother reached over and took hold of my hand. She squeezed my fingers until the bones cracked; but I did not scream out, or otherwise let her know that I was in any kind of pain myself, which I wasn't. We simply lay next to one another, and waited; for what, I had no idea. To make the time pass, I listened to the sound of my mother's trembling, if that is what it was; and I smelled the Posner hair dressing she used waft up, like sweet-scented steam, into my burning nostrils. This was grief, I thought, after a long while of not thinking. *Nothing but grief.* And it ran in my family just as in other families, and in families beyond our own, too. Even in white families. If nothing else, this was ordinary life. Knowing this was, at that time, a huge consolation to me. And as I lay next to my mother—listening to Phil Wilson reproach his ever-invisible God, a man who had loved my mother as best he could for the better part of my entire life, which was then sixteen years—I closed my eyes and tried not to think of anything: neither of the future nor of the past, but of that moment only. More than anything, it was a moment in which I felt nothing made sense to me, and at the same time a moment in which everything did: especially my father's love for me, which I realized then he had disguised as cruelty, if only because he couldn't afford *not* to disguise it. That night, with an odd mixture of calm and exhilaration rising and drifting about like a balloon inside me, I fell into a deep sleep, and when I awoke the following day, strangely now in my own bed, and with the blankets pulled up to my newly-stubbled chin, I could truthfully say without a doubt that my life had begun.

Congratulations

"HELLO," I SAID, CLIMBING OUT OF BED TO answer the telephone.

It was Mariah, Kurt's wife.

I reached up to the loft and squeezed his foot. It was 3:37 in the morning. "It's you know who," I said.

Kurt rolled his body against the wall.

"One night of peace," he moaned. "One fucking night."

I went back to the phone and picked it up. I could hear her breathing into the mouthpiece.

I said, brightly: "He's sleeping, Mariah. Can he call you tomorrow?"

She began to shout: "You put him on the phone, you hear? You put the coward on."

I pulled the receiver away from my ear. Then, listening, I said: "I'll talk to you if you want. Would you like to try that?"

I could hear a radio on in the background.

Finally, her voice slurred, she said: "I disgust him, don't I?"

I didn't offer an opinion.

"I'm his wife," she said. "I married him for better or for worse. I made a vow before Jehovah. Did you do that?"

"No," I said.

"Then God damn you," she said. "May you rot in hell."

I sat down in the chair at my desk and flipped absentmindedly through a stack of yellow index cards. I had written out a series of vocabulary words in black Magic Marker, and then alphabetized for use with my students.

I thought: You must be kind to her. You must.

She stifled a sob. A song played on the radio, Sade's "Love is Stronger than Pride."

I said: "What do you feel?"

Kurt turned over in the loft bed. His calf dangled over the edge of the unvarnished wood beam. I could just make out the swirling topography on the pinkish underside of his foot.

He called my name, and then, abruptly, began to snore.

Mariah said that she would take her husband to court and expose the two of us. She would see to it that I never taught school again.

"You can't even *have* children," she said. "What can you give him? Nothing. You can give him nothing but your sinful body."

"I'm sorry," I said, trying to keep my voice low.

"Sorry?"

"Yes."

She began to shout again. "You've got everything. But what have I got? A big, fat zero, that's what! I've got zero, Mister."

"What about Kwame?" I asked. Kwame was Kurt and Mariah's nine-year old son.

"Oh him," she said. "That boy thinks his old lady's a witch 'cause she'll do what it takes to save her marriage. Anything. Do you understand what I'm saying?"

"I think so," I said.

"I'm a bitter woman," she warned. "I'd murder your sorry black ass in cold blood and *then* curse your eternal soul."

"Oh, Please," I said. "Just listen to yourself. Stop it."

" 'Stop it,' he says!"

"Yes, stop it. Just stop it!"

She fell silent. I glanced out the window on to a side street. It was dark, and a bit too rainy for September. Squinting, I could see only two barren azalea branches reflected in the smeared pane, like twin antlers belonging to some hunted animal. My landlord had planted the hedges a year ago last fall, when I first moved into the building. But they had never come to much, his efforts. I suppose among other things he also lacked a green thumb. He is an older man, in his fifties and without children. Those first months we sat up late, he and I, swapping personal histories and drinking Harvey's Bristol Cream—like Underground escapees newly arrived to free soil, I imagined. I hadn't wanted to know that he desired me; I'd had enough of that in the city I'd lived in before—or enough of that and not enough of the other. On rare occasions, he began to use his spare key to let himself into my apartment while I slept, crawling up into bed next to me, so that when I awoke he was there. I knew then that I couldn't just let it to go on. I began to bring men home from a bar I frequented, making sure to introduce him. When these men slept over I made certain to leave the vents open, so that my landlord could hear what transpired between these men and myself. But this did not discourage him; he'd still use his master key, now and again, to insinuate himself into my life. There was never anything between the two of us; just harmless talk—the way all people do who are lonely. But I didn't care to move a second time—I was at a point of wanting roots, you might say—and so I simply changed the locks, whereupon I promptly received a kindly worded notice asking me to vacate the apartment. Needless to say, I didn't leave.

It was during this time, at my first PTA meeting as a full-time instructor, that I was introduced to Kurt and his wife. He wore a purple knit shirt and beige linen trousers without socks. Tall and angular, with a complexion the color of moist raisins, he called me 'bro' when we shook hands, and held my eyes a fraction longer than polite custom dictated. In contrast, his wife was compact and fair-skinned, to the point of being able to pass for a white woman had she cared to. Ill at ease and guarded, she already mistrusted me, I sensed; and for good reason. All evening her husband and I were consistently astonished at the parallels in our lives. For instance, we had each studied in Còrdoba as undergraduates, albeit five years apart. And both our parents were deceased. As only children, we were each now alone in the world—perhaps me more than him, I added, referring to his wedding band, to which he blushed and quickly scanned the teacher's lounge for his wife.

Later, over a cup of herbal tea, he said in a relaxed but pointed way that he did not know how to communicate his intimate feelings. That had always been the number one problem for most men he knew. Especially black men. Their wives didn't understand them. Maybe because they didn't understand themselves, I countered. That could be so, was his response, and smiled. But then, he wanted to know, how does such a person—who doesn't even understand himself, because of ignorance or fear of what he'd find out—then go about explaining that self to others? Wasn't such a thing next to impossible? Here, I smiled, and shoved my hands inside my pockets, in an effort to shift my sudden arousal. He was asking me, of course, to rescue him. I told him that most men would do better to just say whatever it is they're experiencing at the moment, to simply give *spontaneous* voice to it, in the straightforward and guileless way that my fourth-graders did. To sing—as a poet had written—the body electric.

At the end of the week, Kurt telephoned the school to thank me for the advice, and to invite me to a Spanish restaurant for dinner. He paused, then added: Provided, that is, I was free. I accepted without hesitation. Once at the restaurant, we sat across the table from one another like school kids: alternatingly staring, and dropping our chins. Finally, he began by saying that I seemed at peace with myself. He could learn a few things more from me, he confessed. And to repay the debt—that is, if I had no objections—he could treat an underpaid public servant to an expensive dinner now and again. Say, yes! he urged. Knowledge, after all, flowed in both directions; it was a reciprocal process. He could be my student, too.

I laughed, and the sangria we had ordered went to my head. I touched his hand on the red table cloth. I didn't mean to, but I also squeezed it.

"My brain," I told him, "feels like a bowl of jalapeño peppers. Isn't that strange?"

He held my eyes with his.

"Say what you feel," he said. "Is that what you feel?"

I tried laughing again, but it sounded false. "Well, then," I responded. "Put that way, I guess it is."

After a few minutes I heard Mariah blow her nose. That she had remained silent for so long unsettled me. It became agonizingly clear, just then, what power one person could, with hardly any effort, wield over a second, or over multitudes. Like a lover, or some sort of charismatic leader, I was a little in awe of myself for convincing someone of Mariah's character to trust me, if only for a few moments. I wanted to climb into bed next to Kurt and surreptitiously slip my arm around his thick waist, as my landlord had done to me, perhaps to reactivate his own lapsed faith. Then, it had been a small thing really. No one was hurt, least of all me. But it just hadn't felt right. Not like now, with Kurt. Above all, I wanted to smell his scent to remind myself that he was with me because he wanted to be, and not because of anything I had done to influence him, to lead him on.

I said: "Mariah? Talk to me."

"Give me a break," she said. "I could be hit by a truck tomorrow and it wouldn't be any skin off your sorry ass."

Her hostile tone startled me.

"In fact, your conscience would be clear then, wouldn't it? I'd be out of the picture and my little boy would be free to live with my husband and his fag lover. It's what the kid wants. But what does he know? He's only a child. He has no idea of how vicious adults are. We eat each other alive. Like cannibals, we fill our guts and then move on to the next victim. You're no different."

I crossed my legs at the ankles and rubbed my eyes with the back of my hand. Leaning forward, I saw the twin azalea branches, like a radio antennae, flare up, sleek and white, as a motorist's passing high beams illuminated the window. I knew my landlord was somewhere out there—green thumb or no—watching.

"Sometimes," I said, whispering, "we hurt the people we love most without intending to because, well, because above all we want to be happy. It doesn't matter if other people are happy too. Not one bit does it matter. Just as long as we are. Do you know something, Mariah? Kurt makes me very happy. Sometimes I think that I would do anything to keep him with me, so that I'll be happy always. Or until I'm dead and under the earth, at least. I hate that I have to hurt you because Kurt makes me happy. I hate it. Do you understand me? But I can't afford to think about that. I'd die if I did."

I was sweating under my arms and behind my knees.

I said: "Look, here. I've no right to talk to you like this. None at all. Maybe you should do whatever it is you feel you have to. I can't stop you. It's a free country."

"No!" she shrieked. "It isn't free! We're all prisoners, goddamn you! Every one of us!"

After an extremely long pause, I said, "You're wrong, Mariah. You have to be. But if it turns out you're right, then I don't want to know that; I'll fight knowing such a thing till my last breath. Because if it's true that I can't ever be free in this world, if that's so, then I'd hate that most of all. I'd hate it."

"Fuck you," she said. "You can't hate anything because you've got what I haven't. You're a selfish pig for complaining for what you have. But Kurt isn't like that. That's why you want to take him from me. You're a pig. I guess it's true that opposites attract. Pigs and human beings. I never understood it until now. It's all a game. It's like there's a rope in the middle and Kurt's pulling on one end and I'm on the other. No, I *was*, Mister. Now you are."

She turned off the radio in the background, or maybe the station went off the air.

"None of us is unique," she said. "Like everybody else, I'm fighting knowing what I know already, what I can't help knowing in spite of myself: that my husband has left me; that he isn't coming back; that— that—. But now *I'm* complaining, right? Hmph. I guess my time's up. He's supposed to be yours now. Well, well, well. Congratulations."

"Please," I said. "Don't talk like that."

"*Oink, oink*," she said, and then she began to sob into the phone.

I held the receiver away from my ear for a moment and just stared at it.

She said: "I could feel it happening. Feel Kurt pulling away from me, a tiny bit each night. In itsy-bitsy steps. Like he was a midget in a circus. And then our little boy kept talking about his new teacher that we just had to meet. Then we met, the three of us. And now this. Oh sweet Jehovah!"

I sat upright in my desk chair and tried to focus my attention on Kurt's steady breathing. After all, it had been the simple reciprocity of two lonely people desiring one another that had offered me this conditional release from the penal colony, I thought, to borrow both her and Kafka's grand metaphor for this crazy world. It was true that his wife hadn't mattered, nor had his child. Even Kurt didn't matter—not really; not as much as the rare act of love itself had mattered in granting me this freedom, however fictitious it was. Or was this, too, simply like all the others? Desire only, without Love—which was…what? It no longer mattered. Because beyond this, there was a nightmarish void I knew all too well. I could not go back to *that*. No one could make me. Not even her.

"I didn't stay on this phone to be insulted," I said.

She began to laugh.

"Eventually he'll leave you too, then," she said. "You aren't selfless enough to hold him. Your selfishness will drive him away, just as mine did. But you can change. There's still hope for you. Not for me, though. It's too late for me. I've lost my chance with *him*. I've lost it."

Her voice rang out: "*Oh, god!*"

Gently, I replaced the receiver and unclipped the jack from the phone, disconnecting the line. I thought: She doesn't know her own husband, let alone me. How can she say those things? *The jealous bitch.*

In bed I lay next to Kurt. But I dared not touch him, for a fear, deep down, of what his wife suspected I knew, but was afraid of admitting to myself, rising up and strangling me. I thought: But I *don't* know what it is I know. *No one does.*

Now and again Kurt would stretch out his arm and position it so that I could sense its heaviness lying across my body, across my stomach, say, or my jutting hip. He whistled through his teeth in his sleep and sometimes he spoke as if in phonetic transcription—in aspirates and loud, obscene, bilabial utterances. In an absurd moment it occurred to me that I should leave the country. Like Joseph K., I ought to be made to travel to a small, anonymous city, where no one, either past or present, knew me, and as a punishment—because, at bottom, I refused to know something I knew—where I would be insufferably alone. I had my willful ignorance to be forgiven, I thought, before I ought to be allowed to love another human being.

I looked over at Kurt, his lips moving, the irregular crease down the middle of his forehead widening like a gully, then, without warning, all of a sudden, narrowing yet again, like a thin, obsequious line that stretches to the end of the world.

During the night I got up and sat at my desk. I took out a blank index card and wrote out my name in large black script with the same Magic Marker I used for my students' vocabulary lists. Arranging those cards which had on them printed the words: Loud, Proud, and Shroud into a kind of triangle, I placed the card with my name on it in the center. I thought: *This is who I am.* Then I wrote: *No, this is*: and drew the gluttonous face of a pig next to the letters.

When I had finished I looked up and saw Kurt staring down at me from the top of the loft bed. There was crust in the corners of his eyes from sleeping, and his moustache stuck out from his lip. I didn't know how long he had been watching me.

"What time is it?" he asked, yawning.

"Nearly six, I think."

He patted the mattress with the heel of his hand.

"Come on back up here, bro," he said. "I want you next to me a few minutes longer."

I turned the index card face down and clicked off the desk lamp. The too sudden darkness caused a brightness to flash momentarily on the surface of my eyes, and I had to shut them. Blinded, I stumbled up the ladder and into bed. Kurt pulled my body close to him and kissed me on the back of my neck. I stiffened.

"You shouldn't let her get to you," he said. "This isn't your fight, it's mine. Okay?"

"But maybe she's right," I said, feeling my back grow hot against his chest. "Maybe I am the devil and I should rot for my sins. After all, you have a little boy to think about."

"Sssh," Kurt said. "Go to sleep. My wife doesn't know everything. Why I'm here, for instance. I told her, but she won't believe it. She can't. Such a thing's unimaginable to her. My loving you. But that's not my problem, or yours."

He was silent for a moment. I felt his heart beating against me. I sensed it speed up as my own sped up. After a while, its rhythm adjusted itself to match mine, which was in chaos itself and resonated so loudly I feared it might explode.

"I don't know whose problem it is," Kurt said, finally, and in darkness. "All I know is that I'm where I am. If it wasn't okay I'd leave. I'd pack a bag and go back to my wife and kid."

From behind, he clasped me by the shoulders.

"I would, wouldn't I?"

"I don't know," I said. "Would you?"

Kurt squeezed his arms about my chest.

Struggling, I turned to face him. And in the dark we clutched one another—two hunted people.

I opened my nostrils and inhaled.

"Kurt," I said, my face twisted. "Just hold me."

This Man and Me

Some day I shall rise and leave my friends
And seek you again through the world's far ends,
You whom I found so fair
(touch of your hands and smell of your hair!),
My only god in the days that were.
        -Rupert Brooke (1887-1915)

I HAVE BEEN IN LOVE ONLY ONCE. I was twenty-one years old and lived in the city I think of sometimes as my pretend birthplace, though I was not born there. That city was small and clean and architecturally pleasing to the eye. I can close my lids and picture the slender cherry blossom trees, tall and pink-colored, lining the wide avenues; the Tidal Basin, and the two great rivers calmly opposite one another—the Potomac and the Anacostia—where my father sometimes went to fish. There was, I recall, an abundance of sunny days, people smiling, and the nostalgia of quickly changing seasons. I remember nothing but happiness in that city; though to be sure there were sad times, too. But these I can't recall as clearly.

In that city, because neither this man nor I had money, we often took long, rambling walks. Our shoulders now and again bumped one another, and the hair on my bare arms stood up and tingled. Some days we would stop at a sidewalk café and ask for a table in the uninhabited rear, near the toilets, and split the cost of a large, wet fruit salad. He fed me from his fork and I was promptly awed by his attentiveness, and, too, by the strange, new fluttering taking place in my body.

When he and I were together there was, when I walked, always a hardly perceptible, springy layer of cloud between the soles of my shoes and the hard, weather-beaten pavement. At night he would lay me on his single mattress and hover in the air above me. Often I would forget to breathe. I would leave my body and from a distance watch him trace the outline of my face with the sweaty tips of his fingers. He shoved a digit up inside a still nostril and withdrew an index hung with mucilage. He bit into my flesh until my body would jerk.

Downstairs, hardly out of earshot, his aged mother sat drinking can after can of Piels beer. She wore what appeared to be the same hairnet over her graying head every time I saw her. And her toothless jaw caved in under the despairing burden of what horrified me to imagine could be a person's memories. His weight lay pressed upon me, and I thought, as in Whitman: *This is not only one man!* His tongue lathered my lashes so that I could not see but with my body; it was as if I was surrounded. I could hear the television in the background: *Rowan and Martin's Laugh-In* or *Maude.* It was this soundtrack of canned, vertiginous hilarity which punctuated my moans of pleasure, of gratitude, and simple lust. The fitted sheet on his bed was like his mother's hairnet, always the same one whenever I visited: a shade of dullest white with thick whorls of brown waves in the pattern. Smeared upon this threadbare fabric was the proof of our bond: there, mixed in with the undulations and food stains was his gummy semen mingled with my own, and the dark, oily excrement fart or fucked out to exhaustion from both our saliva-slickened bodies.

In the middle of the night he would awake to find me gazing at his uncircumcised penis, amazed at the now calm sheathe of flesh which had been, only hours before, violently chafing against the inflamed walls of my rectum. Sometimes, when he had to urinate, I asked if I could hold this warrior for him, pull back the shield of foreskin and guide the stream into the bowl. For some reason he always declined, amusement in his brown eyes. I thought, self-praisingly: *My love is so large and uncontainable that it will, sometimes, simply burst out with the most aboriginal of requests.*

Months later, because of the nature of his work, he told me of his plans to relocate to this other city. I did not know yet what kind of a city it was, of its reputation as a murderer and a cheat, as an unconscionable liar. And so I asked him to take me away with him—away from the cherry blossom trees and the wide, forking rivers; and because I was young and persuasive enough in my argument and I humored him, and because he loved me, too, I think, he did this.

The apartment we moved to was directly opposite a small park. But the trees had not grown of their own accord—I could tell this; but rather they were planted with questionable intentions by what seemed to me a vain and desperate city. I could never look at those trees without feeling a slight discomfort in my chest. At the beginning these trees were pruned regularly by a man in a dull-green, belted jumper. Under the pretense of rendering an aesthetically perfect landscape, bandages were wrapped around certain limbs to direct the growth of the branches. I thought, indignantly: *This would never have happened to the venerable cherry blossoms in my city.* In every way these trees were being prevented from flowering into the full extensions of their true selves. This horrified me, and yet I averted my eyes and behaved as if such oppression could not concern me.

However, it was at this point that I began to hold my love for this man more and more loosely in my grip. Other men caught my attention. I would stare after them, smile, and once caught I would snatch my eyes away quickly in embarrassment. I did not understand my own behavior and when I was alone with the man I lived with I would lavish more and more attention upon him, to make up for having strayed earlier with my eyes. But whichever direction I faced there stood before me always this implacable guilt. I turned and I turned and I turned my head until a kind of terror shook me.

"I'm lost," I thought.

Avoiding those trees, I began to leave our apartment when he was away and I would walk along dark streets looking strange men in the eye. If ever anyone exhibited the slightest interest I would panic and accelerate to a brisk pace. I only wanted these men, for an instant, I told myself, to witness my impossible interest in them. I played my eyes over their bodies until I sensed their arousal, and then, like a shot, I would bolt. I never wanted these men to respond: for then I would be committed to them instead of to the man I had come to this city devoted to, and I could not risk such a betrayal.

During those days we seldom had friends over. But when they came this man I lived with would become suddenly more vivacious and brighter than he was when with me alone. I did not take offense to this. I enjoyed the many variant angles to his persona. With him I was always surprised and always, simultaneously, on the surest footing. In honor of the arrival of these people in our apartment he would drape colorful African cloth over his dark chest and sit cross-legged on our murex purple carpet and tell funny stories, gesticulating with his blunt, flat-tipped, expressive hands. White candles in tall cylindrical jars would be lit throughout the room and soft music would play on the turntable: Peabo Bryson or Brenda Russell, singers he liked, and whom I liked because he did. This man was in the theater and so were many of these friends. I was outside all that. I had once been inside but, in the end, he and these people I thought were more committed, not to mention more talented, at this type of work than I ever hoped to be; and, anyhow, I felt the need to uncrowd them all by stepping down and out of, what seemed to me, their already too immense and over-populated circle.

After a while I began to unbuckle my trousers on some of those walks I made at night and stroke my penis to erection. Sometimes, if it was cool, I carried a jacket to drape over me in case of an unsympathetic passerby, or a woman. I lived in an exalted fear of being seen by one of our many friends, and of them reporting back to my lover my nocturnal habits. In my worst hours I craved for this to happen. In time I grew very brave, and often some man would stop to chat with me. He and I would stare at one another, each waiting for the other to grab him where he was most elongated; and both of us, too, incorrigibly lusty, full of a secret, exhilarating, nasty, dual fright.

The city was at its ugliest during this time; it was even common to see grown men taking a piss in full view out on the sidewalk. Besides, the buildings were all covered with soot and in various states of disrepair. Access to the sky was severely restricted by the ludicrous height of these block-shaped edifices. Each morning a new rash of killings covered the headlines. When I returned to our apartment, if this man had come in I would tell the truth: that I had been out taking a walk. Or else, shamelessly, I would lie. During the night I somehow would lose sight of these wanderings and by the morning the memory was all but obliterated. At rest all those hours, next to his dark, regenerative body, somehow this absolved my soul: for he never judged me, or otherwise gave indication that I was not to be trusted. I felt it was therefore incumbent on me not to disappoint him. As in the beginning, by sunrise it was as if I had died and been reborn all in the long, purifying interval of night giving way to the diurnal. I became my old innocent, sweet-natured self: a bit irascible but harmless. I rolled over to him and we made love, or we simply kissed one another upon our fat, ancestral lips, and the trial began all over.

One evening I met a friend of his, a certain actor from the south who was not very attractive. He was tall and absurd with his body—the perfect hick from Hicksville. He spoke with the customary twang in his voice, and always leaned forward to clutch a person on the shoulder when talking. I remembered he had one of those highfalutin society names, as from a Henry James novel: Charles or Frederick.

It began simply enough. I loathed him. He had no sense of moderation and saturated himself in musk-scented body oils. He reeked of it. Instead of making him more desirable, this repelled me. But then I felt badly for him. He so wanted to be a part of the 'in' crowd, stylish and in the 'know,' like the man I lived with, and all the others in his profession—those who paraded themselves in bright plumage and behaved as if a camera were recording their every gesture. He reminded me of myself: the outsider who longs desperately to be inside but who simply does not fit; who isn't popular or even talented, or especially well-liked, but who is merely tolerated as the embarrassing love-object of one in their ranks; who has simply *lucked* in on a certain crowd, as I assumed I had with this man and his friends. After a while I could not stay away from him, or he me. We phoned each other and confessed in quick, movie-scripted voices:

"Don't you want me?"

"He'll find out."

"But you want me, right?"

"No."

"*Liar.*"

At his apartment we circled each other. He had already bathed himself in his favorite scent and it was all I could do to keep from retching. To my horror, he wore a short-sleeved, plaid shirt a size too small and loose-fitting generic blue-jeans with loopy stitching on the back pockets.

"No," I thought, when he held me. He did not remind me of myself, but rather of boys I had gone to school with, boys I had admired yet had not been friendly with since they claimed a much stronger kinship with girls. Nevertheless, that first time he exuded caution for only an instant. Soon he bruised my neck with his uneven teeth and I had torn a button off his shirt. In no time both our jeans lay undone at our ankles and we ground our bodies together, liberally, as if to reach the core of something we both believed lay concealed in the deepest recess of the other. He did not have as finely muscled a body as the man I lived with. His was of a larger mass, it's true, but it was soft and there was a surprising opacity to his copper complexion; it did not give, but took. In our lovemaking there was no confidence: it was all crying out and mad panic, as though we were sure the world would end because of our illicit groping. And yet I knew it was too late to turn back, nor did I really want to.

Some nights I lay next to the man I lived with and did not know him. I was twenty-three or twenty-four years old and had grown skittish. I began to hide my various new faces from everyone who entered our lives. When friends visited I discouraged them from staying long by storming out of the room, or by showing them the door when I decided enough time had lapsed. Leaving, they merely smiled at one another and said, "Oh, Mark's just being Mark. Isn't he cute?" I had lost my identity and I resented these people for telling me who I was when I didn't know myself, and when they'd gone I would become an emotional gymnast before that man; it was as though I'd gone mad. He was calm and loving, and sometimes he would say my name aloud to cool me off, or sit astride my body and ride my erect penis to exhaustion; other times he would take up his sketch pad and draw mythical figures of tall, redbone men with scales along their backs and a bit of schizophrenia in the eyes.

We never returned together to that other city, the one we had left. He often went alone to visit his aged, alcoholic mother and I would wait for him after my nights of walking the streets. I had adapted too well to this new city. I misplaced all memory of the parades my mother had taken my brothers and me to see every year along Constitution Avenue, for the cherry blossoms. I forgot the picnics on the grounds of the Smithsonian. When I was with some other man, and not the one I lived with, I would be caught off-guard sometimes by a recollection. A vivid sadness would wash over me and I would drift back in time to when he and I would ride the Metro from the housing project where he lived with his mother into the center of that historic city. He would sit next to me and just as the doors closed he would shut his eyes. I sat in silence beside him, awed by his trick of blotting out the world through meditation, as I had been awed once by his fork between my lips. This mastery of myself was what I wanted, but I could not be confident that I would ever come back from such depths; therefore, I leaned upon the proven solidity of his frame for support and guidance instead of searching for it from within. I thought: *I dare not risk such a journey for fear of losing myself inside my vast, chaotic self.*

When I was twenty-five or twenty-six he came home from being weeks away and confessed his love for some other man over me. This was in the summer, and while he had been away I had undergone yet another transformation and was more determined than ever to hold my love more firmly in my grasp. I had not seen that musk oil-wearing actor for some while, or any other man. I had been cleansed this time not by his presence but by his very absence. It left a hole in me the size of that city which had initially nurtured our love, and I had stared bravely into it while he was gone. The depth of it stunned me; I did not want to ever be without him. I could not, I thought, survive it.

We tried to wait it out. When he left in the evenings to rendezvous with this other man I would fire up sticks of incense to burn the stench of jealousy away. I played his favorite records over and over like a mantra, especially "If Only For One Night"—a song he had serenaded me with in our courtship. I would extinguish all the lamps and, with a single white candle, sit in that heavy darkness and try to glean from Brenda Russell's mellifluous voice and, too, from the guilt I felt, what could be salvaged from my shattered world.

Eventually, it was no good. One night this occurred to me and I lay up in our loft bed, sobbing. The windows were opened and all our neighbors could hear the despair flying out of my body like birds being freed from an aviary. We had often laid there ourselves listening to the desperate fucking, and the curses in English, but in Spanish too, which was the language of that part of the city. For seven hours the deluge was unceasing. The man I loved lay listening in the next room. I did not know to what extent he was aware of my small infidelities, but I was sure that this was the very reason that had pushed him, finally, to form this sudden alliance with another. The planet had abruptly come spinning off its axis and was now shockingly out of control: I had not truly imagined that this could happen, no matter how often or rarely I strayed. If anyone, I thought, reminded me of those adolescent boys from my youth—in whose bony arms I once imagined lay my eventual salvation—it had been him all along; and yet for years I had felt that I was suffocating with him, and that simultaneously I was living the greatest pleasure a man could fabricate out of the stuff of his dreams.

Later that summer I moved out of the second floor walk-up he and I had shared in that city into a one-bedroom affair across the bridge. I did this decisively, and yet in spite of my packed boxes I could not quite believe in my own actions, or in the actions of those few friends who helped me with my belongings. It was not my body, I told myself, that this was happening too, but some other poor man's worn-out, adulterous body. I was now very much like those trees standing across from our building, I thought, who had suffered, in years past, a similar asphyxiation. Like them, I felt paralyzed at having my potential for love smothered so early in life, without having so much as a say in the matter. I shut my eyes to what seemed a ruling beyond my self-government and, instead, I fashioned an alternate reality to compete with the obviously untenable one that faced me. For months afterwards, and then for years and years, I convinced myself that as far as those trees were concerned, the filthy pieces of sackcloth would eventually rot and drop from around their bark-covered bodies, and with a vengeance an unprecedented blooming would occur. In my patience I willed for a similar reconstitution of justice to happen for this man and me. I clung with fingers and nails to the hope that if I were patient and good—something I had not been before, but had wanted to be and failed—then this man would forgive my indiscretions and, because he had once loved me, come back to me.

After all, he was my god.

A Type of Vampirism

I CANNOT RELEASE MY SOUL, INHABITED AS IT is by the ancestry of this relationship. The dance floor is not crowded since it is barely 10:30 p.m. Paul is trying to rub his butt into Calvin's crotch while the three of us make like Celia Cruz and get down with the Latin funk. Calvin and I are the color of brown semi-gloss paint and hail from a southern region of the planet; only Paul is different: he was born and raised in Rochester, New York. And being so alert, I am conscious of men everywhere attaching significance to our body movements. Paul gyrates in the center, between Calvin and me. His own rhythm is off the mark, but it is the only way that he can participate on this level with the two of us, so what can you do? I'm sure the image he projects is hardly flattering, especially since the club is predominantly his kind to begin with.

What a sight we three must make: two stunning native men symbolically surrounding this ultra-pale boy-king with the magazine cover smile and pointed nose that is too straight. Vicariously through Paul, they are worshipping the ultimate sexual fantasy involving our trio, though it will remain a sublimated lust they would never admit to, even if tortured. But what does it matter? I know the real story without their true confessions—I see the infrared drool slipping discreetly down from their mouths, as they watch us; I see the loose alabaster of their little necks quivering. However, Paul is making a mockery of the self-control they all aspire to by his inept dancing.

To set the scene, Paul and I rendezvoused at Uncle Charlie's for drinks after work. Once there we simultaneously spotted a young Sidney Poitier-type straight from *A Patch of Blue,* pondering his fate over a Miller Lite.

At Paul's urging I invited him to join us. Between 7:30 p.m. and 9 o'clock, we managed to finish off two and a half large Margaritas in half-gallon pitchers. I pissed most of the tequila and lemon juice out through my urethra; our new friend, who admits to being from Gainesville, Florida, perspired his away dancing. But Paul, my lover for the past hundred years, has not used the rest room since we left our apartment, and one does not sweat easily the way he dances—if anything his pores are clogged. Therefore, he is hardly in control of the Wall Street stoicism the majority of his people have in common, that *GQ* calm, that cold, plastic mannequin indifference the menfolk of his tribe attempt to perfect everyday of their lives. So he continues to rear-end his butt into Calvin's crotch, living the moment for them; and needless to say, his comrades are embarrassed, being so shamelessly exposed within the territorial markings of their own club.

I place my palms along my thighs and lower my manhood to the wood floor, penis meat flopping around behind the zipper of my jeans, sweat falling suggestively down the fabric making everything moist and identifiable. I want them all to go mad and dribble at the chin. It is the least they deserve for flaunting such dazzling celestial brightness and tempting me in those early years before Paul came along.

This exercise keeps me preoccupied while my lover seduces Calvin. If I did not have fantasies to hold me in check then I would be a very dangerous individual. Calvin is the one I need to wake up to in the mornings now. It is a conclusion I've just reached here, under these colorful, hypnotic lights that illuminate the whimsical and distort whatever is left. Paul is disappointing me because of his typical behavior. In the beginning of our relationship I had hoped he'd be different from the collective somehow. But he is and he isn't. What more can I expect? "Swept Away" by Diana Ross plays, and I think how it is my favorite song in the universe. But I've lost all enthusiasm because I can't have what I want. Like a pouting child I stop dancing and lean over to Paul and shout into his ear that I'm sitting this one out. The floor is too crowded for me to enjoy myself, I tell him. I can't be free! As I saunter past, the brother from Gainesville looks at me and I can only smile at him, unwilling to elaborate on the situation so early in the evening. Of course, by deserting him in the middle of the refrain I am jeopardizing any chance of enlisting his aide. But if he cannot read in between my polite and very timid smiles, the smiles that say, "Rescue me, if you've got the balls," then what more can I do? The rest has to be up to his consciousness. Polite smiles are the way we weaker men of color get over the hump of our existence. But, self-admittedly, it has become a habit for so long—these smiles—become security that it is about all we trust when out in the world. Among our own we should want to lower the masks we use as shields and be joined, and not so easily fooled by a man's impressive dental work.

Because of the lyric in the song more ethnic types are dancing. But life is hard and then you wind up living forever; so what's it all stand for?

With a dramatic toss of my head, I storm off the floor just as Ms. Ross takes off into her own equally futile world of fairy tale, albinistic lovers—the only men in our star system who could possibly leave her so out of breath all the time.

It numbs me when I think of how much we are alike, she and I.

2.

As we leave the club I am holding onto Paul by the waist and he is nuzzling my neck, his blond hair so soft and deceptively innocent it irritates my skin. Calvin, tonight's unknowing savior, keeps a slightly more cautious pace behind us. My lover is even more intoxicated than I diagnosed and begins to bump and grind against my hip bone as we walk, still apparently hearing the bass tones in the space between his ears.

It is September 23rd, a highly humid Friday night in Lower Manhattan. All evening Calvin and I have avoided showing too much of an interest in one another. It makes the clientele edgy when minorities congregate in public places; and I'm sure, being from Gainesville, Calvin is sufficiently well-read in the language of race relations not to unintentionally upset the precarious equilibrium of the times. After all, he is a Negro like me, a spade, a volatile punching shadow to be wary of—he knows that ideally we belong with our own kind anyway. Why, then, in the face of so much mass rejection, are we still unable to mate without all this red, beige, and blue tape? This cultural bonding is necessary for our people's mental health, especially now in the 80s among so many Sushi bars and young urban types, like my lover Paul. If we don't eventually find one another in the aftermath, then what was the past for, the hangings and rapes, the spoken-word poems and burning supermarkets?

Calvin begins to whistle and Paul reaches out his anemic arm to him in a beckoning gesture. Calvin submits and allows his hand to be held onto and squeezed. Funny…all we need now is an unbiased photographer interested in the facts, who will not distort what is obvious in favor of a paid-off, sterilized version: with my prep school Oxford sleeve strangling Paul's neck and him disco pumping against my underwear, and Calvin being dragged by the wrist behind us like someone's domesticated pet, the bulb flashes—or might flash. It would make for a perverse lampoon on a modern preoccupation: the glorification of submissiveness as an exalted state.

Paul is losing his balance as we walk, and I am largely carrying him and pulling Calvin along as well. Considering it is not yet midnight, I suggest we stop and compose ourselves before going further. Paul has begun to snore on my shoulder and does not respond. I twist my neck to face Calvin for his thoughts. It will be the only time I've acknowledged him all evening without using Paul as a go-between. But somehow he is now walking in front of us and the back of his head faces me. I use this opportunity to imagine that the tight curls are villages, and the shape of his hairline, the continent Africa. I want to shrink myself and live among those other inhabitants who surely must dance naked inside there. It is where I belong and the place sensation suspects I originate from. I watch the breath rise through Calvin's shoulder blades and feel both expectant and intimidated waiting for him to respond to me without my lover's involvement. (O, how September's air and this young, would-be warrior I've been seeking for so long are unthawing the frost of my own tribal memories!) Finally answering me, Calvin motions with his protruding forehead in the direction of what has to be some hallowed ground where sacred rites are performed. "Christopher Park," he saying, shifting to face me and pointing. "You know, across the street from Sheridan Square. We can rest there if you like. It's close by."

Without speaking, I nod my head. It is all that I can give him now with Paul so close to me. The three of us cross 7th Avenue, two invincible creatures, tall, strikingly elegant in our attitudes, supporting this fragile boy-man from America on either side of us. A blood-red station wagon full of teenagers with loaded muskets runs a red light just to taunt us; but our feet are too agile from racing ostriches in the midday sun and we reach the sidewalk with our own time to kill, which we selectively do, and never just for the sport of it. Normally, when I am with Paul, it would be my instinct to yell obscenities; yet tonight—maybe because I am here with the man I hope has come to save me—the impulse dissolves, and is replaced instead by a comforting nobility, an aloofness. Through this transition Paul continues to sleep, his saliva beginning to burn a hole through my Oxford shirt. Calvin slides an arm down from my lover's shoulder to his waist, where my own arm is positioned. It is here that our undecorated skins touch for the first time; we did not shake hands during introductions back at Uncle Charlie's, nor did the two of us shake our booties anywhere close enough for it to happen on the dance floor. A delicious frustration has been building for the benefit of this moment. Finally, after so many impostures, I somehow sense Calvin to be that young tribesman sent to deliver me back after all.

We follow the moonlight in search of a bench with the least pigeon shit to scrape off.

Upon finding one, Calvin helps me with Paul, whose eyes are now revolving wildly up inside their sockets. He sits down on the left and I on the right. Paul is of course in the middle between us, asleep. His teeth glisten like fangs off the starlight dusting our bench. And not bothering to conceal my own lengthy incisors, I open my mouth and inhale a deep breath of this glorious night air and yawn widely. Calvin, the profile of his face exposed, is silent and cocks his ear to the wind that is faintly blowing. I find myself envious of the strength I notice in his jawline: so straight all the way nearly past the cartoonishly angled cheeks. This feature lends a certain history to his appearance I find lacking in my own since I've been with Paul all these decades. Not that I've always been without it, mind you: this arrogant expression of indestructibility in the midst of wandering souls and death everywhere. It's just that of late I've become more sensitive to internal fragility as the most natural enemy to living a long life. In fact, to keep myself firmly rooted in the here and now these days, I close my eyes and press against the lids with my strongest fingers to re-discover all over again the delicate workings behind my every breath. But there seems to be no way possible I can even hope to avoid spiritual obliteration inside this unsafe body, the way the world is. And whatever higher purpose I have to fulfill, it appears, is being slowly siphoned from my bowels by the strain of optimism in this very relationship with Paul.

As if vomit were dripping from my lips I say to Calvin: "Just look at him. Of course he's able to sleep without fear in this park. He's like a human night-light, for God's sake!"

Calvin lowers his eyes from the dark sky and affixes them to me. This way his thoughts will be mine and vice-versa. There is no need to bullshit each other, no need for roundabout conversations to get things said. He reprimands me for my lack of trust where he is concerned. After all, we are the same, he tells me—or is it that I imagine him telling me this? The concept of fear springs largely from the reincarnated bones of subjected peoples and is not as detectable in those who will surely come back as rodents, or worse, dishonest men of power who, towards the end of earthly life, will suffer like hell! An animal scurries in the bushes behind our bench, possibly a rat. Paul moans and mumbles the closing argument in his stupor. In a trance, he whispers: "I desire your soul.... Your greasy, mahogany, biscuit-flavored soul..."

A street woman appears on the scene and walks towards us. To me, she resembles the woman on the pancake box: the same roley-poley body and checkered scarf tied round her head. She drags a torn shopping bag along the ground. When she gets closer she stops and stares at the three of us and tries, it seems to me, to pull our individual faces up from her memory. My impulse is to scare her away by saying "Boo!" or something at least as adolescent. But instead I free myself from Paul's body and reach for my wallet. And since we are thinking with one mind, Calvin duplicates my actions. Again, the rustling in the bushes. Paul moans. And before he can give us away Calvin expertly thrusts his tongue down my lover's throat! The street woman is, of course, perplexed and tugs at her head scarf. In the end, she refuses our generous offer and fades back into the park scenery. When she is gone, the bond between Calvin and myself has grown thicker. We smile, and can now fully acknowledge and commiserate over what is common in both our lives. I ask him if he wouldn't mind helping me get Paul into bed; the rest I imply through the inflection of my voice, not to mention a little body language. Calvin says, "No, Bernard. Don't mind at all. My pleasure," and stretches his left arm up under my lover's back and we leave the bench and pigeon shit to hail a cab instead of taking the filthy "A" train to Brooklyn,

It is here that our fingers intertwine.

3.

In the elevator, Paul wakes up. He is at his most adorable with sleep in his eyes. In fact, it is the only time I can get a decent erection with him these days. His skin has the most coloring then because of the way he sleeps: all curled and tense like a fetus. How can I hold an unborn thing responsible for past events? When the alarm rings in the morning I feel the need to protect him since he's hardly fetal and cannot be blamed and, therefore, I *must* transform fear, somehow, into love if I am to face the day at all. And of course Paul merely lies flat on his back while I see-saw atop him, venting myself, justifying our various happy vacation photographs together, twisting his pretty, rosebud nipples and giving full voice to the screams I try to let out only when alone with him.

Calvin is leaning with one hand against the elevator door, his eyes assembling facts from what looks to be semen stains on the floor tile. Paul slides up to me and begins to lick at my neck. I stroke him behind the ear and restrain the swell in my jeans since it is nowhere near the cock's crow. The doors open at the 13th floor and the three of us exit. Calvin is first among us and steps into the hall and waits.

"To the left, Calvin," my voice directs him. "All the way round past the exit sign. Paul and I live in apartment 13S—'S' as in...plantation."

Without undue emphasis meaning is conveyed. He does what I intend for him and receives enlightenment through my eyes. Paul is no doubt aware of this exchange between us. But he has occupied himself with the hairs growing like wire from my chest, so Calvin does not notice his silent participation. Anyway, my lover likes the abrasive violence of scrubbing his skin against my pecs; the purple irritation his face shows in the morning when he wakes redeems him in a similar way that my

screaming fits redeem me during our love-making sessions. When we get
to the front door of the apartment Calvin is already there, waiting. He is
not watching me any longer, but is studying Paul and the obsession he has
with my chest. I insert the key inside the lock. Paul has begun to perspire
and soon will be too sober to let me keep this unbalanced power of mine,
as it were, even though on some occasions I think he'd like me to. I twist
the key and the front door swings open into a cavernous room. The lights
are out when we enter and the familiar darkness gives me the courage
to reach out for Harriet Tubman's imaginary hand for reassurance. Paul
leaves my side, gliding across the room, and one by one ignites the three
dozen or so candles we have placed throughout the apartment, his skin
beginning to lose color and glow in the flames. Calvin shifts his weight
onto his heels when he sees this and starts to wobble slightly. It is a heady
experience the first time a man of Paul's caste is seen under the spell of
candlelight; his reaction is therefore to be expected. But if he is to be my
underground railroad tonight then he must regain control and rule it, and
not be swayed by Paul's showy exhibition. I slip my last free hand under
Calvin's spine and hold him steady. Finally, Paul glides down the hall
and disappears into the bathroom to shower. Instead of perfumed soap
we bathe with Ivory because it professes to keep skin incredibly soft and
young-looking through years and years of constant use.

When I can hear running water, I pivot and feverishly grip Calvin by
the shoulders and pull him in towards me.

Calvin's natural scent makes me long all the more for tropical Africa
and the kola nut, for the photographic world of Leni Riefenstahl and her
Nubian tribespeople-turned-fashion models and their gray-white ash
bodies, so sacred and pure and since birth kept separate from me. I see a
ceremonial dance being performed in front of dilating pupils. I hear hand
claps spelling out my newly chosen name in rhythms I am surprised, yet
overjoyed, to be familiar with. In the distance, lined haphazardly along the
mountains, chimpanzees flail hairy arms to welcome me, their humanoid
tears creating a river in honor of my returning that will nourish a land.
Calvin doesn't resist until I bury my nose even deeper in his neck.... It is
then that he struggles. But I am over the edge now and all-powerful and
dig my lengthening nails into his back. The two of us fall to the carpet,

and in order to increase my delirium I bite into Calvin's shoulder, and when I do he knees me in the groin and I roll off him onto my side, with his flesh underneath my fingers. He gets to his feet and stands over me to deliver his only speech of the evening, his African skin smeared red, the pockets of his chinos turned inside out, his eyes murderous. But the words he wants to spew out at me are subordinated beneath a really awful Richard Pryor impersonation, and the only thing I hear that makes any sense is:

"Damn, brother! What *is* your motherfucking problem?!"

When Paul rushes in Calvin is already out the door and into the elevator with, what I imagine he supposes are, my defeated semen stains staring achingly up at him from the floor—and for all I remember of my recent past, they just well might be. My beautiful translucent lover, his body still damp from the shower, bends down to me and warms my cheek with his own. His voice is tired, but as always after these nights out he nonetheless asks me if I want anything solid to eat before going to bed. There is some fried chicken left over from my one-hundred and twenty-sixth birthday party two months ago that some unknowing youth prepared. It wouldn't take any time at all to re-heat. Also, there's a little salad left as well. I need to eat, he says, telepathically, especially if I am going to take rejection so close to heart. I'm looking weaker with each encounter. Maybe if I didn't come on so looney tunes things would go better for me. If I were more patient, maybe. Less desperate. I shake my head violently. I cannot bear his compassion tonight. Malnutrition is setting in. I allow Paul to take my hand and lead me into our sleep chamber for renewal, for rejuvenation, for rest. As he kisses me goodnight I am reminded of the enormous pleasure I feel while in his arms, and the sense of safety his touch imparts, and again I fight it. Fight him. If only I could be happy with Paul, if only I could be swept away, like Diana Ross, by a white man's empathy and love for my tribe. But it does not ever seem to be enough, Paul's devotion to me, to black people. History, like a gigantic, vindictive wheel always catches up to me, no matter how far ahead in the game I seem to get. Perhaps this is why Ms. Ross has so many white men in her music videos. Maybe she thinks the quantity helps to compensate her for the years these men ignored her, downplayed her truly unique beauty because it was different from what they and their great grandfathers knew beauty to be.

An animal scurries in the potted bushes we keep out on the terrace— possibly a rat, possibly a thrill-seeking God bored with His life in Heaven.

Paul lays an arm across my chest and moves in close to me. "I'll love you through the fires of eternity," he whispers into my ear, his breath a toxic vapor. "I'll love you even if one of these days you get your coward's wish and evaporate into the air, you crazy man." I look up into his blue eyes and tears begin to cascade down my cheeks.

He and I will stay like this until sunrise, or until the alarm clocks governing the galaxy announce the start of a new day. Until that time, we will continue to awaken each morning and consume one another's physical essences before beginning again the circular dance that defines his life and mine. But, for now, the three dozen or so candles lighting the apartment will protect our fragile and troubled spirits from drifting too far apart, from disintegrating, from exploding into the already too dense atmosphere surrounding this godforsaken planet.

You Must Change Your Life

MICHAEL COLLECTED HIS SHOULDER BAG FROM UNDERNEATH ONE of the theater seats, where he'd hidden it, and went into the men's toilet. He took out the damp cloth he'd brought and soaked it in hot water. He began to soap his genitals and pubic hair very thoroughly; then he rinsed the cloth and wiped himself dry.

When he came out of the men's room the man with whom he'd just had sex was waiting for him in the theater lobby.

"What's your name?" he asked Michael.

"Tim," said Michael. "And yours?"

The man extended his hairy hand. "Cal."

Michael shook the man's hand; then, leaning forward, he kissed him lightly on the cheek.

"I have to leave now," said Michael. "Work tomorrow."

The man looked at his wristwatch, then at Michael.

"Christ! It's after 1:30."

Michael shifted his bag onto his shoulder. "Yeah, I know."

An awkward pause followed. The ghosted images of the actors on the screen flickered against the man's face as Michael watched him.

"I'll walk out with you," the man offered.

Out on the street the cars whirled down 7th Avenue. Michael pursed his lips and glanced surreptitiously at the man who said his name was Cal, though at first Michael didn't believe this was the truth.

They waited together for the signal to change.

Finally, the man asked: "So which subway do you take?"

Michael, caught staring, jerked his eyes away.

"The 'A,'" he said. "Uptown. You?"

"The 2 or the 3. But I'll walk a bit with you. That is, if you don't mind?"

"No," Michael said, shaking his head, although if truth be told he did mind.

From the passing headlights, Michael noticed flecks of grey in the man named Cal's thick dark hair. Michael was a 'hair person,' and in the theater he had eagerly run his fingers through the bushy hair of the man who vigorously sucked him. The man who called himself Cal. Now and again he'd open his eyes to see...Cal's mouth, like the mouth of a tiny fish in a bowl, opening and closing about the mushroom tip of his erect penis.

Michael actually pictured this, as the two of them crossed Barrow Street.

He noticed too that "Cal" was appraising him. Turning his profile a little to the left, then to the right, Michael smiled.

"What's so funny?" the man asked, also smiling.

The two were shoulder to shoulder.

"This," Michael said, surprising himself and smiling sheepishly. Like he did when he was a high school student. "Meeting in a place like that. It's not what you expect, I guess."

The older man quickened his step, and now slightly ahead of Michael, he turned back to look more directly at the younger man.

"What do you expect? Usually, I mean."

Michael felt a passing stiffness in his shoulders.

"I don't know," he said. "Maybe nothing. That's why I'm surprised. From the first, I expected something with you."

"Really?"

"I didn't know what. Just, you know...something."

At Sixth Avenue, the man touched Michael loosely on the upper arm.

"I'd like to see you again," he said, in a rush of words. "Is that do-able? If not, I understand."

Without hesitating, Michael tore out a page from his journal and wrote out his first and last name, and his true phone number.

"Sure," he said, and handed the paper to the man named Cal, who all of a sudden beamed and himself looked boyish, though he was easily in his late thirties or early forties.

"My surname's Richards," he said.

Michael motioned to the slip of paper in the other man's hand. "My name isn't Tim. But I guess you figured that out."

"No," said the man, looking down at the torn paper. "I hadn't."

"Oh."

The two shook hands, and parted.

* * *

On Saturday, Michael and Cal went to see an off-Broadway play. At the intermission, feeling uncertain, Michael said he had to go the bathroom. But he quickly left the theater and didn't return.

The next day Cal telephoned. Listening to the messages Cal left on the answering machine, Michael thought: No.

He immediately contacted the telephone company and had his listing changed to an unpublished number.

Over the next several weeks, he avoided the theater on 7th Avenue. Instead, he frequented an adult movie house along the Westside Highway. Open 24 hours a day, Michael took to visiting at odd hours. Sometimes he wore a fedora; other times he pasted on a mustache he had purchased at a costume shop in the east village. He dressed in attire he normally abhorred: corduroy trousers, a tie and sports coat. A pair of eye glasses.

Once, a man he had met through a personals ad asked Michael to screw him dressed in the leather chaps he had spied in Michael's closet.

He didn't once run into Cal.

At the end of the summer, the company for which Michael was employed sent him on a trip upstate. After checking into his hotel, Michael walked across the street to a family-style restaurant and ordered dinner. Adjacent to his table, he saw a man who looked like Cal sharing a bottle of wine with a very handsome, younger white man. Upon seeing him, the other man, very discreetly, but very sharply, turned his back to Michael.

Cal! Michael thought.

In bed, that night, Michael recalled the incident. The other man had aged. His hair had grayed even more. Nor was he as good-looking as Michael had remembered. In fact, that was why he had left the theater so abruptly that afternoon: Cal wasn't attractive enough to him to risk what he was considering risking. In order to take such a risk—a risk, in fact, no one else would take—a man had to exceed all previous boundaries of personal attractiveness. Cal, being ordinary, didn't exceed this. It wasn't Michael's fault, then. Or Cal's. So why should he feel culpable?

When Michael had concluded the round of meetings for which he had been sent to oversee, he checked out of his hotel. At the checkout desk he saw Cal, apparently also checking out.

"Hi, there," Michael said.

The other man, turning in his keys to the woman attendant, nodded.

"Good morning," he said.

Michael followed Cal out into the bright cold air of Albany. He touched Cal lightly on the upper arm.

"Remember me?" he said.

The man turned around, squinted his brown eyes, then said, a bit coolly: "I'm sorry. Have we met?"

A taxi pulled up to the circular driveway, where Michael and the other man stood. Getting out was a short, round man in a yellow striped necktie and bald head.

"Oh," said Michael, instantly horrified that it wasn't at all Cal he was addressing, but a stranger. Now that he considered it, this man didn't even resemble Cal.

"Sorry," he said. "My mistake."

Michael hurried to his rental car, a powder-blue sedan, and drove to the airport.

* * *

Back in the city, Michael searched for the man named Cal's telephone number, which he had casually written on a post-it and (or so he thought) slipped inside a drawer. But he couldn't find it.

He tried then to recall Cal's surname. But he couldn't remember it. Was it Thomas? No, that was someone he had met and slept with months earlier.

Soon, Michael began to return to the theater on 7th Avenue. Although he did not admit this to himself, he hoped in fact to run into Cal again. To facilitate this, instead of donning a disguise, he dressed as himself: no hats or scarves; no phony hair pieces.

He'd take a seat at the back of the theater. This way, his reasoned, he would notice who entered or left.

He saw everything. Nothing escaped his scrutiny:

An older man, dressed in a leather jacket, a jockstrap and scuffed Fry boots, stationed himself outside the men's toilet. Whenever anyone entered he'd wait a few moments, then he'd follow behind them. Almost immediately, whoever went in came right out again, and a few seconds later, so did the old guy in the jockstrap.

Another man, this one younger (maybe twenty-five or so), a Wall Street-type, always showed up at the same time each day and took up the same seat, four rows from the screen, two seats in from the aisle. He wore a stiff Burberry trench coat and carried a briefcase. He'd sit for fifteen minutes, and then walk upstairs; two minutes later he'd come back to the main level, look around, then go to the basement. In another two minutes or so he'd return to his seat. Fifteen minutes later he'd repeat the ritual.

Few patrons, Michael realized, actually had sex with anyone. He'd been one of the more active men. And being black, he was of a course a commodity in such places. Over the years, Michael had thankfully concluded that the majority of men who frequented adult theaters were white. Upon seeing him in a bar, many of these men would not so much as look his way. Here, however, away from friends and "family," they readily made known their eagerness to drop to their knees before what they assumed was his "gargantuan" member. Such men he usually ignored. However, sometimes he would tease them by letting them get a momentary glimpse at his erection while he stroked it in his seat, or stood at the urinal, pretending to take a piss.

The irony was that Michael did not, in fact, have an overly impressive penis. But in the darkness of the theater, and with the insatiable desire these men exuded distorting their judgment, it hardly mattered. They saw not what was there, but what they *imagined* was there. Here, the shadows worked distinctly to Michael's advantage.

With Cal it had been different. Also a black man, he hadn't pursued Michael; but it was Michael who had pursued him.

It happened this way: Cal had been sitting where he was sitting when they had first met, in the rear of the theater, where he could survey the entire scene. He had been dressed in a pair of light-colored slacks—khaki's, Michael recalled—and a dark blazer; a white crew shirt underneath. And he wore a small ring that glinted on his pinky finger. Michael had passed him several times that first evening, without the other man so much as flinching. Once, imitating a Mapplethorpe photograph he'd seen, Michael had taken out his half-erect penis and let it dangle suggestively between the teeth of his zipper. Still nothing.

That night Michael went into the men's toilet and jacked off. When the old man in the leather jacket and jock strap followed in behind him, out of meanness, Michael let him stay and watch. Once, the old guy tried to get near enough to touch Michael's cock; however, Michael snarled theatrically, so that the man backed off.

It took going to the theater several weekends in a row and seeing Cal that first time before the older black man would acknowledge his presence. Finally, while Michael was running cold water over his face, Cal walked into the men's room to relieve himself. Sensing his chance, Michael stood at the urinal and, to his astonishment, saw that the man was actually urinating!

He wanted to laugh, but he held back. When the man was finished, he tucked his still flaccid penis back inside his pants. He turned to Michael, whose face went blank, and asked if he knew the time. Michael shook his head. He wanted to say more; he couldn't. Finally the man, his eyes hazel (*hazel*, of course!), said to Michael:

"You have a beautiful dick."

"Thank you," Michael said, feeling momentarily self-conscious, as if he were speaking to his father; but still his hand fell reflexively to his groin.

He pulled on his penis until it lengthened.

"I'm not very good, I'm afraid," said the man. "I mean, I haven't done this sort of thing very often. Some, but not a lot. If you don't mind, I'd like to try on yours, though."

Michael was so taken—focused instead on the flushed feeling in his chest rather than in his balls—that he nearly lost his hard-on. He nonetheless had the presence of mind to begin backing up into the stall behind him, whereupon the man (whom Michael thought was even better looking than Tim Reid, an actor from the television show *Simon & Simon*) soon followed.

Out of a sense of duty, the guy in the jockstrap kept watch outside the stall door.

That was how the two men had first met.

* * *

Weeks had passed since Michael had returned from Albany and he still had not chanced upon Cal. He began to wonder if he ever would again.

Friends telephoned and invited him out; he always declined. On nights when he wasn't at the theater on 7th Avenue, Michael remained in his apartment, stroking the Playbill from the off-Broadway show Cal and he had attended together.

He became a reader of books: Rilke. Baldwin. Jean Rhys. Gide.

One afternoon, passing a stationery store, he decided to purchase a daybook to record his thoughts and feelings.

He wrote the following as his first entry:

> Exactly when it happened I can't be certain. But when I was twenty-two or twenty-three I began to notice that people were essentially false with one another. Seldom did anyone say what he or she really meant. Or do what their promises said they would do. In fact, more often people meant just the *opposite* of what they said, and did just the exact *opposite* of what they promised. If I hadn't figured out the pattern I'm

sure it would have taken me longer to understand things than it has.

Not that I understand things now; I don't. But I'm at least aware that people are liars more often than they tell the truth—to themselves as well as to others.

I hadn't known such a thing before I was twenty-two or twenty-three, or else I had forgotten I had known it—which can sometimes happen, I suppose. And for good reason. Who wants to know that no one of us can be trusted. That faith is a completely make-believe concept, a fiction, a hype. That each person is alone in the world. And that other people will do everything they can to discredit you, to undermine you, to make you look foolish. Surely, no one wants to know such a thing.

At least, I don't.

But after a time writing proved too disorienting, and Michael gave it up. He turned to sketching, but realized he had absolutely no aptitude for it. Sometimes he played his dad's old blues recordings and tried to sing along, but that too proved a failure. He hadn't the fighting spirit.

He had stopped going to the theater altogether. He had no desire to be stared at by strangers; to be groped and sniffed, like some kind of perishable food. Nor did he have any vindictive need to see other men debased, as he imagined many of the men who were regulars at such places—as he had been a "regular"—were debased.

In time, Michael began to deny his very body.

Friends remarked on his lost weight. His cheeks became drawn and hollow, so that his lips, always full, now seemed larger and out of proportion to the size and shape of his face. Winter came, and Michael stayed indoors for long stretches of time, rummaging through drawers and closets, searching for a slip of paper on which he had long ago written the telephone number of someone important. But who? Both the person's name and face eluded him now.

Michael's thirty-third birthday arrived. His mother sent him a Hallmark card, with a lengthy letter, updating him on the family news. He read it silently to himself, a frown lingering around his drawn mouth.

"What tiresome people," he thought, and threw the card and letter into the trash.

One morning Michael caught sight of his reflection in the window at Macy's Department Store and nearly tripped over his feet. Who was that person?

He called into the office: "I'm not well," he told his assistant. "I'll come in when I can. Phone me if anything urgent comes up."

Of course, Michael feared that he was dying. It was only fitting. He had lived a perfectly self-interested life. So why not die? There was neither wife nor children to provide for; no lover to grieve over him and give him comfort. These things had eluded him—or rather, over the years, he had shrewdly managed to dodge them all. Once he might have married the woman with whom he'd been involved in college: Cynthia Patterson. But then Rob entered the picture, and Cynthia was pushed out of the frame. And a bit cruelly too, he recalled. After Rob there was a succession of men. Men whose taut bodies and equally taut temperaments were, in this lustful context, so startlingly new to Michael as to rouse what must have looked, to observers, like a perpetual fever. And then came Jamie— sweet Jamie, who, though only twenty-three, was really too young and too innocent for Michael, only twenty-seven himself at the time, but who felt he had already lived the vicissitudes of a much older man. Poor Jamie. He had meant it to be "forever"; that was the expression Jamie had used that first time they'd had sex—no, "made love," is how Jamie preferred to describe it. And of course it *was* love that he had made with that boy, Michael remembered, stretched out on his bed, as he was, waiting, a bit too theatrically (which was his way) to be claimed by the great white Father—whose name was God.

But it was not Death that came, but someone else.

Having heard that Michael was ill, Rob Starks boarded a plane from Indiana, where he taught religion at a Catholic university, and arrived to New York City, on Thursday, February 3rd. When Michael saw his former lover he figured he had already died and, as a formality, was simply now having replayed before him the whole footage of his reckless and self-absorbed life.

Robert, 5'8" tall, clean-shaved, with straight light brown hair, a diabetic himself, nursed and cradled Michael for nearly two months—until spring. At that point, Michael's mother, from North Carolina, along with his Aunt Lucy, took over her son's convalescence. The doctors Rob and then Mrs. Strayhorn had consulted, all agreed there was no medical reason why Michael should be ill.

Once again, however, Mrs. Strayhorn posed the one question they all feared, and which Rob had at first suspected. The resounding answer, all around was: "No, ma'am. There's no evidence of the virus in your son's body."

His Aunt Lucy sighed, "Thank God!"

By the first week of the following summer, Michael had regained nearly every ounce of weight he had dramatically, and unexpectedly, lost. Speaking to Rob over the telephone, Michael endured the latter's chastising of him:

"Goddamn it, Mike! How'd you get that way? What's eatin' at you like that?"

Michael couldn't answer. He scarcely knew how. He stared in the mirror at his new body and face. Of course, they weren't exactly new: it was his old body and his old face. Simply, they had been away on a trip, but now they both had come back to him. And he was glad. It surprised him to realize how happy he was to be among the living. So many things and sensations he had never before valued. He found himself holding a loaf of bread, trying to balance it on the tips of his fingers, while simultaneously smelling the clean grain flavor. He stared at a blank sheet of typing paper, marveling at the fibrous threads upon which words, held merely by dark ink, in turn acquired so much power.

Then, pulling out the journal he had purchased months ago—it seemed a lifetime, really—Michael recalled his half-hearted attempt at writing. He read over what he had then written. And the past returned to him—all of it—in a flood of regret and pained feeling.

He blurted aloud the name of the man for whom he had nearly given everything.

"*Cal*," he said. "*Cal*."

He recalled how, seated in the theater on 14th Street and Broadway, he had turned the playbill over in his sweaty palms. Cal, turned away from him at the time, was dressed smartly in a pea-green summer suit, and brown, wingtip shoes. At one point he shifted to Michael and pointed out a famous personality who was also in the audience that afternoon. It was all just so perfect for Michael: Cal's company, the weather, the good feeling in his chest. Of course, it was what Michael had always wanted. What he could have had with Jamie if only he had *believed* in it as Jamie obviously had. The rightness of the afternoon filled his whole body. *Oh! Oh! Oh!* he had wanted to shout.

Then, straining to stare into the side balconies, Michael caught sight of a man from the 7th Avenue theater—someone whom he had once let... let touch him.

Just then, his whole insides gave way and he found that he couldn't breathe.

At that moment he leaned over to Cal (handsome, respectable, "I'm-afraid-I'm-not-very-good-at-this-sort-of-thing," Cal), and excused himself to the men's room. "I'll be right back," he said, smiling, though he knew he wouldn't.

Instead, Michael ran. He ran through lower Manhattan, terrified that on whichever street he found himself that life of his would follow him and unmask his secret life to the world. All of it. *Those hats, those scarfs, those ridiculous slivers of* adhesive hair!

Back at his apartment Michael barricaded himself in. He didn't deserve someone as good and clean as Cal. As gentle and polite. And what was worse, he hadn't yet sucked Cal's penis. Or kissed his mouth, even. He'd stood against that filthy tile wall at that filthy rundown theater and *taken*, as he always had, failing—though this time he had wanted to—to give back as good as he'd gotten. To fall to his knees and drop open his mouth and.... And what?

And *love*.

* * *

Over the next several weeks, Michael went about in a kind of beatitude. People who saw him commented that he had never looked more at peace. That a grace lay permanently stamped upon him as a result of his tussle with death. At the office, his co-workers marveled at his recuperative powers, hoping that if they were ever afflicted themselves a similar inner conviction would pull them through—that, and of course family and friends.

Michael no longer frequented those adult theaters, not that he disparaged those who did. How could he? After all, not everyone is caught as he was. Some are luckier, some are less. It was no longer his concern.

But Michael never did forget Cal. He never saw him again, it's true. But, as it turned out, he remembered this man for the rest of his life. It was the least he could do.

Between Us

Like so much else, people have...misunderstood the place of love in life, they have made it into play and pleasure because they thought that play and pleasure were more blissful than work; but there is nothing happier than work, and love, just because it is the extreme happiness, can be nothing else but work. —So whoever loves must try to act as if he had a great work: he must be much alone and go into himself and collect himself and hold fast to himself; he must work; he must become something!

—Rainer Maria Rilke
(1875-1926)

DEAR M—:

It's Tuesday morning, 11 o'clock. Last night I stayed in Harlem at Shari's apartment. I arrived at 6:30 pm and she and I talked for seven hours, until almost 2 am. We hadn't seen one another since the end of summer, when I returned to Wheaton for the fall semester. So much has happened between us. Your name came up during one stretch when Shari and I hit on the subject of relationships—of loving and being loved.

You don't know this, but Shari has been involved for nearly two years with a woman, after years of being involved only with men. This woman's name is Jonique, and one day she'll be famous; we're sure of it. Jonique, you see, is a hip hop/jazz artist and a few weeks ago she signed with a Warner Brothers label, the same one Madonna records on. Just a week ago, Shari tells me, Prince even telephoned to congratulate Jonique, and to tell her that she plays a "mean bass." Just a week earlier Jonique had appeared on NBC's *Saturday Night Live* as the musical director for the group Arrested Development. Shari had recorded the segment on the VCR, and just last night she replayed it for me. The success for Jonique is new, but her talent is not. She's highly regarded in the music industry for her virtuoso ability on a variety of instruments. But Jonique is young, and though she displays a wisdom beyond her years in some things, there's still much that she does not know about herself, or the world. She and Shari have had a battle of a time together. Believe me, I could tell you stories! Jonique has medical problems that may undermine her burgeoning success, though: she's an epileptic; not only that, but I believe there's a tumor in her skull that needs prompt attention. This Xmas Shari and Jonique, are going to Andover, Massachusetts, to spend the holidays with Pat, Shari's sister, and her husband, David; Ma and Pa Carpenter, Shari's and Pat's parents are also coming up from D.C. A family affair, you could say. It was in this context that I told Shari about the essay you wrote in the November issue of Notre Dame's independent monthly, *Common Sense*, where, among other things, you talk about a broader definition of what family means, or could mean, for those of us who are lesbian, gay, or bisexual and who may not have told our families about our sexuality. You write:

> I've spent enough time involved in gay politics and in the gay rights movement to learn how often the energy and anger behind storming homophobic barricades come not from the power base of a loving relationship with family members, but from the rage built up after so many years of self-estrangement from grandparents, parents, sisters and brothers.... While we are in the process of appropriating the freedoms possible in an openly gay life, gay folk need to take some time away from the neighborhood, family, and childhood friends whose familiarity drove us close to despair. As in all major transitions, we had to leave the people for some

space to think about and experience the issue [i.e. our sexualities]. But when this liminal period is over and new relationships built, it is imperative that a connection be made to the before-life. Otherwise, the responsibility for the breach remains with the person who left and it will continue to "drink up part of my breath for the day" (W.S. Merwin) until the reconnection is made. Even if the family's rejection is virtually assured, the truth must be shared so that the responsibility is shifted from the person alone to the family, whose members can talk it out with one another. Often great relief accompanies the admission. Yet, even if the family reacts badly, we can then accept that there was indeed little to lose and much personal freedom to be gained.

I like what you have to say here, M–. Although there are current tensions in Shari's relationship with her parents, I think she too realizes how important and necessary it was that she tell her parents about Jonique, and who she is to her. So far Shari's Mom is the most uncomfortable about the issue; her Dad is willing to discuss the newness of it all, and the shock and hurt he felt when Shari first told them over a year ago. In the interim, Shari sent her parents some literature to read on homosexuality— pamphlets, letters, a book. As you mention in your essay, hers was one of those "major transitions" we all go through periodically in life. And by offering her parents information on her sexual orientation, Shari was doing exactly what you suggest lesbian, gay, and bisexual people ought to do when sharing such new knowledge, that is, specifically, "to leave the people…some space to think about and experience the issue." This Xmas season, then, for the group of them, will be an attempt to restore balance by jointly participating in an event they all had shared in the "before-life," as you call it.

I like that coming together of families. As Shari and I talked last night, this issue as to my own long estrangement from my family—in particular, from my brothers and father—struck hard. In the way that I congratulate my friends for their perseverance in maintaining a bond with *their* families, I realized that I don't always practice what I preach. In other words, I'm a fraud, M–.

Here's an example for you. A couple of nights ago I had a dream from which I awoke in a panic. In the dream I had been having sex with my brother, Kerry, the middle brother. After I reached orgasm I rose from the bed and scurried to the bathroom. When I came out again—this is all still the dream, mind you—I could see into my parents' bedroom. There, seated on the bed, I saw my mother's father, my grandfather, lift up a newborn. At this point I woke up, and realizing that I had ejaculated in my shorts, quickly went into the bathroom to clean up. Back in bed, next to Allen, who was staying over, I felt embarrassment and shame at having a wet dream at my age. I resolved not to tell anyone about it, not even Allen, to whom I tell most everything. Later, however, unable to make sense of the dream I did tell Allen about it. He offered a very plausible interpretation: Because I seem to feel that most connections I make with other people are through sex (I had confessed this to Allen on another occasion), it was obvious to him that I was attempting to form a bond with my brother in the only way I knew how. The image of my grandfather (who had recently died) and the baby was meant to represent, Allen suggested, a new beginning of sorts—a passing away of old ways of relating, and a birth of something new. As Allen put it, my subconscious self actually desired a more productive relationship with both my brothers, but my conscious self steadfastly refused this as an option; hence, the troubling wet dream.

I told Shari about this dream too, and about my good friend Allen's generous reading of it. As I've already mentioned, it was a very long evening for the two of us. A lot came up, especially about my own particular tendency to keep other people—or rather my insistence on keeping them—at a distance by drawing these people in close but then, seemingly in the very next breath, harshly shoving them away. Much of this behavior stems from my childhood, I know, but some of it too—just how much I can't be sure—is a product of forces that I feel my family and I were born into as African Americans. I had been rereading some stories by James Baldwin, I told Shari—particularly the story "This Morning, This Evening, So Soon," and so my mind, as I spoke last night, was swirling with images that weren't entirely of my own invention. Baldwin says so much in his writing that resonates with me. The story itself is narrated by a middle-aged black American expatriate who achieves a measure of success in France as a singer and film actor. After a number of years living in Paris he meets a Swedish woman, herself a kind of expatriate, I guess, and the two promptly fall in love, or so the narrator thinks. See, having lived so many years in America, as a black man, the narrator isn't sure that his ability to judge other people, even himself, isn't a little impaired. One night standing on the Pont Royal bridge this man and his girlfriend, Harriet, quarrel, and the narrator realizes, at that point, that the way he views the world and himself in it has been altered drastically, and for the better. He says to the reader:

> There were millions of people all around us, but I was alone with Harriet. She was alone with me. Never, in all my life, until that moment, had I been alone with anyone. The world had always been with us, between us, defeating the quarrel we could not achieve, and making love impossible. During all the years of my life, until that moment, I had carried the menacing, the hostile, killing world with me everywhere. No matter what I was doing or saying or feeling, one eye had always been on the world—that world which I had learned to distrust almost as soon as I learned my name, that world on which I knew one could never turn one's back, the white man's world. And for the first time in my life I was free of it; it had not existed for me; I had been quarreling with my girl. It was our quarrel, it was entirely between us, it had nothing to do with anyone else in the world.

This passage has particular relevance for me, especially where you are concerned, M–. Years ago, you and I had a similar quarrel, except that our quarrel didn't occur on a bridge or in a foreign country. We were at Hunter College on 68th Street and Lexington Avenue, in New York City, at a reading by Essex Hemphill, the editor of the recent volume *Brother to Brother: New Writings by Black Gay Men*. I have a story in there myself, remember? Anyway, Hemphill was performing, which he sometimes did in those days, with a percussionist named Wayson Jones. A number of my friends were also in attendance, people you had not met previously, nor had they met you; these were mostly black gay and lesbian people. As always, you and I were particularly affectionate that evening. If you recall, we sat in the aisle at the very front of the auditorium; I sat behind you with my arms around your waist. It was a tense night for me, maybe for you, too, meeting so many of my friends and being one of the few white people in the hall. Allen was there, as was Ralph—remember him? I think our quarrel actually began with Ralph, because of my attraction to him. (Let me say now that it wasn't an attraction to which I was truly committed; simply, that night Ralph became, for me, a kind of lifeline, and as the evening wore on I clung to the kind of safety I imagined he represented for me, a safety that I imagined you couldn't represent—couldn't (oh, I hate to write this) because you were white). I loved you so much M–. It was a kind of love that lifts a person out of himself, and makes him less self-centered than before, when he was alone or with others who understood even less of themselves than he did. I don't know who I had been before I met you, M–. As you know, you were my *second* love, after Stanley, and that, I feel in retrospect, is much more difficult to achieve than one's first, which comes at a person when he isn't looking, and which knocks him down and imposes itself on him whether he is ready to be imposed on in this way or not. However, after first love has come and (in my case) abruptly and cruelly been snatched away, a person isn't quite sure that love will come for him again. He trusts less, after all, and isn't love just that, a matter of trusting more and more each day? In the case of first love, it isn't a question of blindly giving in to trust, I don't think—one's whole self, body and spirit, is already so anxious and needy that to give in is the least of one's concerns. If anything, with first love it's a question of how *much* a person gives in, how hard and how far he's going to fall when that person he's giving himself to—whether man or woman—reciprocates, says *Yes!* at the same exact moment he utters *Yes!* himself. Then the both of you collapse heart-first into the other, sated at last. *That's* first love.

(Turgenev has an entire novel—it's very short—on this very subject.) On the other hand, it seems to me that *second* love isn't anywhere near as reflexive. After first love fails, disillusionment, like rigor mortis after the heart stops, sets in. Few have come back from beyond *this* state, and those who have come back, through being medically revived or through some other divine means, have fantastical stories to relate. It's no different, it seems to me, with second love.

Forgive me this long set-up, M–. I want you to realize how deeply I value you, and the relationship we forged, and how deeply I felt, and continue to feel, the loss of it in my life today. Losing you was my error. But it was an error that I was in no way prepared to avoid making in 1987. I didn't know myself well enough in those days; I didn't know the world well enough either. Above all, I didn't know in what ways my relationship with you—a black man and a white man (*there*, I've said it!)—would reverberate in that world. And did it ever reverberate! That night at Hunter College was my first sense of the outrage such a relationship as ours could trigger among other people. I had grown up in predominantly black neighborhoods as a boy. I had heard things, really horrible things, other blacks said about whites and blacks together, but I had never heard those things applied to me. That was all the difference, and I'm ashamed to say that I simply caved in under the blunt force of that language, M–. Even Allen, my dearest friend, a man I love more than I love my own flesh and blood siblings, joined in the general chorus of condemnation, remarking at one point that evening, "Mark, you can do better than that," meaning of course, "Mark, you can do better than trolling around after white men, who aren't worthy enough partners for us royal and resilient black warriors." I'm sorry for having been so weak for not being able to resist the looks of reproach I saw in my friends' eyes that night, M–. I had not known what to expect; truly I hadn't. And so after Essex's and Wayson's performance that night, when everyone gathered in the reception area for refreshments and, too, for that all too rare and remarkable thing to occur in those days: black gay and lesbian fellowship, I felt the first pangs of real anxiety I'd had since meeting and falling in love with you. Naively, I had only wanted my friends to be happy that I'd met someone and fallen hard for him. I was self-centered and foolish and so I had not anticipated that they would so harshly judge, even rebuke, me for entering such a relationship. And while I was both horrified and dismayed at them for their rejection, there was also the sense, deeply imbedded but steadily rising within me, that my friends were actually in the right to be disappointed in me, that I *had* really somehow engaged in a traitorous act by giving my heart, to say nothing of my black, royal body, to a filthy, murderous, thieving white man—as all contemporary white men, to us new world, racially correct blacks at least, should be thought of. For that was how my friends, and perhaps not a few strangers, viewed us that evening—not as Mark and his new boyfriend M–, but as a black and white man, in other words: a self-hater and a body-stealer. I, who by virtue of my race and sexuality was one of them; I alone belonged to their group, whereas you were the interloping antagonist in their—which is really our nation's—little drama. By choosing to align myself with you, M–, it was as if, to these good people's offended eyes, I had stepped through the proscenium, walked up the aisle and out of the auditorium's doors into the street. I'd closed the show, so to speak, but the passion play had not yet reached it denouement. It was when I realized this, however dimly I had perceived it at the time, that I felt a sudden immediate desire to detach myself from you as quickly as possible. It was a reflex, mind you—in other words, on some level what my friends felt I too umbilically felt, though I didn't live it as radically, as with as much remote hostility perhaps, as they did. Nevertheless, I began, at just that moment, to seek my way from you. And so there was Ralph. Mine, though, to be sure, was hardly a pure attraction to that young, exquisitely handsome, nut-brown-skinned *Afro*-American man. In the end, Ralph Wilson was a kind of tunnel I hoped to scurry through in order to make my quick get away from you. I didn't *want* to escape from you, M–, but I felt I *had* to escape or else risk a swift excommunication by my friends, and even from the watchful strangers who were gathered there and who shared our menaced identities and history. On some level I'm ashamed to write this, M–. But on another level I am very proud that I am finally confronting this debilitating shame. After all, I have never adequately explained to you why I behaved as strangely as I did that night at Hunter College, and why this night signaled the beginning of the end of our relationship. "We" were never the same afterwards, M–, and you know it.

Now, all these years after the fact, far too many, I am trying to tell you what happened and why.

Subsequently, the argument that followed, along Central Park West, wasn't an argument between you and me only. As in Baldwin's story, I didn't feel myself "alone" with you on that wide, heavily trafficked avenue; rather, "the menacing, the hostile, killing world," I felt, was between us. It was not our fight only, but the fight of black men and white men that "made love impossible" that night. Dating from that moment on I began to move self-consciously away from you. And I couldn't fight it; I tried, but I didn't have the necessary psychological weaponry at hand. While my life may be very different now, I still don't believe I have such arms. But I'm all the while searching for them within me. People of my sort—blacks who fall for whites—can never know when such combat will be necessary, and so one must be prepared always. Perhaps this is why there hasn't been anyone in my life since you, no one of much significance anyway. For that reason the decision to leave New York in order to finish my undergraduate degree was an easy one: There was no one to consider but myself. And I would be lying to you if I said that I wasn't a little bitter over the whole thing. I think love is a very necessary and valuable way of being in the world. Without it I'm not certain if a person isn't always a bit off balance. Rilke, as you know, says that for one human being to love another is the most difficult task entrusted to us, and from which all other work eventually springs. It's a similar sentiment to the one you expressed in your *Common Sense* article, which encourages lesbian and gay activists to unite "love and anger" in fighting their battles, "rather than out of anger alone."

Of course Shari knows the whole story about you and me. She's my best friend and so I shared all this with her years ago, when I was attempting to understand what had happened between us. I even wrote a story about it once, trying to understand—calling it "A Type of Vampirism." Last night I simply reiterated a few details, to link my pushing you away to the other, equally pressing issue of my general estrangement from my immediate family. Baldwin is an invaluable writer for me because, well, in addition to being black *and* gay, he is so eloquent in analyzing the complexities of what it means to have to navigate multiple identities in North American culture. Simply being a human being presents a whole host of conflicts, but to be gay *and* of African descent in our society only increases the conflicts. Everyday I'm learning more, M–, more strategies with which to combat the various conundrums—a word Baldwin favored—that crop up in my life. Already I've pushed away several people—not only family members. And since I'm not a great believer in regret—it does no good to regret, since every error in judgment is but an invitation to growth—I won't say that I regret having pushed *you* away when I did. True, I've been miserable and lonely, but it is a loneliness that I feel must be borne if a person is ever to know himself and, in turn, to truly know others. I hope Rilke would approve. I hope you do.

Much love,
Mark

Acknowledgements

I would like to extend my heartfelt thanks and gratitude to the following individuals: From Massachusetts, Sue Standing and Jeffrey Banks; From New York and Brooklyn, Stanley Wayne Mathis; the late Dana Rose; Stephen Williams; my best friends Shari Carpenter and Allen Wright, without whom I would perpetually be dazed and lost; to all the writers of Other Countries, those both alive and passed on, for first validating my early attempts at fiction and whose fellowship, warmth, and fierceness helped me to find beauty and strength in an identity that others have often despised. From Philadelphia (now Minnesota), Martin Connell, I'll always be a little "mad about you." From California, Shirley Geok-lin Lim and Dan Jaffe for his encouragement and generosity. From New Jersey, Steve Berman for welcoming me into the fold. From the U.K., John R. Gordon, you inspire and humble me. From Maine, my colleagues in the English Department, especially Dave Collings and Celeste Goodridge; to Mike Kolster and Christy Shake, Olufemi Vaughan and Rosemary Effiom for stubbornly keeping their hearts open to me, and their front doors; to Jill Smith and Jorunn Buckley for recognizing things in me that I don't often recognize, or appreciate, in myself; to John Thurston and our beloved pets, alive and moved on, all of whom have granted me love and happiness over the years, even when—no, especially when—I have tried hard to resist both these things. And finally, to Loretta Fields Foster, my mother, a woman who bore me, nurtured me, and who would never let me stop believing in my possibilities.

About the Author

Guy Mark Foster has published short stories in such places as *Shadows of Love: American Gay Fiction, Brother to Brother: New Writings by Black Gay Men,* and *Ancestral House: The Black Short Story in the Americas and Europe.* He teaches at Bowdoin College in southern Maine, where he lives with his partner of 16 years, two dogs, Fergus and Venus, and a black cat named Kenya.

CPSIA information can be obtained at www.ICGtesting.com
Printed in the USA
LVOW061924280613

340740LV00012B/1790/P